CW00455405

Best K

Best Kept Village

Mart Capsticks

Troubador Publishing Ltd
Unit E2 Airfield Business Park,
Harrison Road, Market Harborough,
Leicestershire LE16 7UL
Tel: 0116 279 2299
Email: books@troubador.co.uk
Web: www.troubador.co.uk

ISBN 978-1-80514-420-5

British Library Cataloguing in Publication Data.
A catalogue record for this book is available from the British Library.

Printed and bound in Great Britain by CMP UK
Typeset in 11.5pt Minion Pro by Troubador Publishing Ltd, Leicester, UK

For family and friends.

Introduction

The district of North Norfolk is famous for its long, golden, sandy beaches, scattered with brightly painted beach huts; its tranquil and quaint seaside fishing villages, staithes, and harbours; and its marshes and dunes – home to many rare species of bird and marine life.

Stepping off the tourist trail and back inland, you will, however, discover an altogether different aspect to this district. Nestled in the sleepy countryside are a myriad of stunningly beautiful villages. The houses and buildings are built in the same local style, with red brick and quintessential Norfolk flint and cobble stonework, all topped with natural clay pantile roofs. In fact, one might say it's the very picture of an English rural idyll.

It is here that you will find the villages of East Barton and West Barton, situated roughly a mile apart, but connected together by the Old Barton Road. This, in turn, connects to the main road running the few miles to the handsome Georgian market town of Holt. Also on the Old Barton Road, exactly halfway between the two villages, lies The Barton Arms – a historic and attractive former coaching inn, now run as the local pub and restaurant.

Every year, the North Norfolk District Council runs a competition to decide which village in the region is the best – by which they mean in terms of both beauty and community spirit. The competition is called 'Best Kept Village' and habitually attracts some thirty or so villages to compete. Over the years, both East Barton and West Barton have won this prestigious award on several occasions, and it has become a matter of great pride for all those involved.

In fact, you could go so far as to say that the villages have become somewhat bitter rivals…

1.

It was a glorious spring morning as Reverend Clifford Rose was doing the rounds of his parishes. Due to falling attendance numbers within the Church of England these days, it was not unusual for clergymen to look after several parishes and Reverend Rose was no exception. He was the rector of three parishes, with seven villages in all – and each village had its own church.

Reverend Rose was a tall, thin man – almost athletic, you could say. He had short black hair, wore brass-rimmed round spectacles, and had a slightly scruffy, worn-out look about him. He considered himself to be a modernist (as far as vicars go, that is) – perhaps even going so far as to say – a bit trendy. This was largely due to him sometimes playing his old, battered guitar during sermons. Like most guitarists, he thought he could play far more melodiously than he actually did, but his parishioners put up with listening to whatever song he chose to butcher with Christian good grace.

He was riding his much-loved antique bicycle and was fast approaching two of his villages, namely West and East Barton – or the Bartons, as he liked to call them. On the outskirts of West Barton, the first property he encountered was Barton Hall. The magnificent hall and estate were owned by Lord Richard Braithwaite. The property had been in the ownership of the Braithwaite family for generations and the property and title had been duly inherited by Richard some fifteen years past. Due to the receipt of a monumental inheritance tax bill shortly after, Richard had been forced to run the estate as an exclusive shooting ground to help pay off some of the debt.

Next to the grand entrance gates, and entirely in keeping with his inflated ego, there was a stunning eight-foot-tall hedge that had been skilfully clipped, pruned and sculptured into huge letters reading:

RICHARD BRAITHWAITE ESTATES

It had taken Richard's groundsmen years to grow and perfect the hedge. It was one of West Barton's highlights for the Best Kept Village Competition and it was Richard's pride and joy.

As Reverend Rose cycled by, a huge top-of-the-range 4x4 came hurtling through the gates, nearly knocking him off his bicycle. As it shot off down the road, a haughty voice could be heard shouting, 'Morning, Vicar!' out of the driver's side window. It was Richard, of course.

The reverend dusted himself down and continued into the village. He bade everyone he passed a most pleasant 'Good morning' and they all responded in kind. In the centre of the village, he happened upon Dr Maryam Jahan, who was busy tending the West Barton flower display on the village green. Dr Jahan worked at a practice in nearby Fakenham, but lived in the village. She was a jovial, kind and caring lady, and a credit to her profession. She also had a passion for horticulture and all things floral.

'A very good morning to you, Maryam,' he called as he pulled up beside the village green. 'What a splendid display you have!'

'Oh, thank you, Vicar,' replied Dr Jahan. 'I'm just making sure everything is looking tip-top for the competition – it's not long now before they start judging, you know.'

'Indeed, indeed,' chimed the vicar. 'Well, you're doing a wonderful job!'

The vicar pedalled off again and soon passed the church. He nodded appreciatively to himself that while the church looked presentable and well maintained, with just a sprinkling of flowers – it did not look ostentatious. He was very careful to remain neutral when it came to village interactions and loyalties, especially with the competition looming.

In the churchyard, he noted Mr Kleeb was at work. Vincent Kleeb was the local funeral director. He was busy making a funerary arrangement from white lilies – a task he excelled at. For some reason, Mr Kleeb always made the vicar feel slightly uneasy. He was a small, wiry man with greasy, thinning jet-black hair. He was very pale-faced and this was exacerbated by his black ill-fitting suit. He had an uncanny resemblance to the *Vulgarian Child Catcher* and when he smiled, his crooked teeth imbued him with all the warmth of a circling sand tiger shark. The vicar gave him a cursory nod, shuddered and moved on.

Towards the end of the village, there was a delightful, pretty detached cottage, to the front of which was a magnificent display of multicoloured tulips. The house belonged to a formidable lady by the name of Cynthia Barrington-Smythe. She was of average build, had greying hair parted severely to one side and possessed a gaze so ice-cold that, like the *Medusa* of Greek legend, she could freeze your blood and leave you motionless and stonelike with the most cursory of glances. Cynthia was chair of the West Barton Best Kept Village Committee (WBBKVC) and took the job extremely seriously. In any situation, she was the kind of person who presumed that she was in charge of everything and everyone. It was very much the case that it was 'her way or the highway', and anyone daring to disagree or waiver from her plans in any way were cut down to size forthwith and in no uncertain terms. She was now retired but had worked in the NHS as a professional nurse and, over the course of thirty years, had bullied, bawled and battle-axed her way through the ranks, reaching her ambition of being hospital matron by the age of fifty. Along the way, she had cajoled a naïve junior doctor into marrying her. After twenty years of purgatory, he had sensibly given up the ghost and was now six feet under – and a lot happier for it. They had produced a son, named Michael, whose main ambition in life was keeping out of her way. A sentiment currently shared by the vicar, who was terrified of her and was now desperately trying to pass by unobserved. He had no such luck.

'Ah, Reverend Rose – I've been meaning to catch you!' came the shrill voice from her doorway, as she stepped out of her porch.

The vicar's heart skipped a beat. 'Oh, Cynthia – good morning. How nice to see you,' he lied.

'I have a favour to ask of you,' she said, giving him her nicest smile. Or certainly what she thought was her nicest smile, but was actually giving the vicar minor palpitations.

'Oh, yes,' he replied, wondering what on earth she could want of him. 'Fire away.'

'Well, you know we have this friendly competition going on?' she asked.

'Yerss' said the vicar carefully.

'Well, I know it's a long way off, but we're thinking of organising a little Christmas party to demonstrate the strength of our community spirit in the village. We hope to make the right impression on the judge, you see, and we'd love to have you attend as our special guest.'

'Now, Cynthia, you know I must remain impartial when it comes to the competition,' he said, doing his best to wheedle his way out of it, 'and I think my presence would not be conducive to the spirit of fair play.'

'Nonsense,' she snapped. 'I simply won't take no for an answer.' She softened her tone a little. 'Besides, we wouldn't dream of asking you to take sides. Of course not. But we did think a Christmas event like this really should have a representative from the church… don't you think?'

Blast, he thought. She had him over a barrel there. 'Very well,' he said, sighing, 'I'll be happy to drop in for an hour or so – but that's all. I'm very busy at Christmas time, you know.'

'Of course. That's very sweet of you – thank you.' She beamed at him, causing him further palpitations. 'I'll book you in then.'

And with that, she turned on her heels and swept back into the cottage, leaving the vicar with the distinct feeling that he'd just been coerced into making a deal with the devil – and a bad one at that.

Hey-ho, he thought. *Onwards and upwards.* He climbed back on his bicycle and headed down the Old Barton Road towards East Barton. Half a mile on, he passed The Barton Arms. The landlords were Keith and Jenny Atkins, a jovial enough couple. They'd run a pub in their hometown of Norwich for many years, but had always yearned for a quieter place in the countryside. They'd bought The Barton Arms only a few months ago and had been pleased with the purchase price. The reverend could see that they were busy taking a delivery of beer, and the drayman was rolling the kegs and casks down a hatch into the pub's ancient cellar. Keith and Jenny gave the vicar a cheerful wave as he passed by.

He continued the last half mile, rode past the colloquial road sign that read 'Slow You Down' and then he could see East Barton's village green and their own magnificent flower display as it hove into view. There was a park bench situated on the green and as the reverend approached, it seemed that someone had left – what appeared to be – a heap of green plaid blankets piled upon it. As he drew closer, he noticed that the blankets moved slightly, and he suddenly realised that this rather untidy pile was in fact a person – Ethel McKinley, to be precise. She was from Stirling, a proud Scot through and through, and fiercely patriotic of her homeland, despite not living there.

Unfortunately, and there is no polite way of saying this, Ethel was not graced with good looks. If you could imagine an ill-tempered, gurning bulldog, all wrapped up in tartan, this would not be an inaccurate description. If the face of *Helen of Troy* had launched a thousand ships, Ethel's would have sunk them. She was a short woman and her figure, if you could classify it as such, was not so much doll-like as dollop-like. Coupled with her unerring dowdiness and air of miserable gloom, even the kindly vicar found her, frankly, to be bloody hard work. Among the other organisations she had chosen to inflict herself upon, such as the Women's Institute and The Salvation Army, she was also on the board of the East Barton Best Kept Village Committee (EBBKVC).

'An exquisite morning, is it not, Ethel?' asked the vicar, who, despite all the odds, had decided to try and strike up a conversation.

'Bah!' came the terse reply. 'It was far nicer in my day.'

A remark that totally wrong-footed the poor vicar and left him struggling to think of a reply. Instead, he settled for grinning inanely, cursing the old bat under his breath and continuing his progress through the village.

Greeting more locals along the way, he soon reached the centre of the village, where East Barton church could be found. Outside the church was parked a monstrously huge American pickup truck. The vicar knew the vehicle was driven by the local farmer, Bernie Rolls, and he could guess why Bernie was there.

Many years ago, there was a small paddock adjoining the churchyard owned by the Rolls family. Bernie's father, Bill, had generously donated the paddock to the village back in 1966 to celebrate England winning the world cup. He'd hoped the paddock would be used by the youth of the village as a small football pitch. As times changed and the population of the village became increasingly elderly, there was no real demand for football facilities, so it was decided to convert the pitch into a bowling green. Bernie had overseen the conversion process himself, being highly skilled at landscaping, and the result was a fantastic success. The bowling green was a finely laid, closely mown and painstakingly rolled stretch of turf – perfect in every way. The bowling green was East Barton's highlight for the Best Kept Village contest and, sure enough, the vicar found Bernie tending to his masterpiece. Bernie was a huge man, six foot four inches tall, and built like a barrel. He was immensely strong, but, like many men his size, he was a gentle giant.

'Hallo, Bernie,' called the vicar over the churchyard wall. He liked Bernie.

'How do, Cliff!' replied Bernie in his broad Norfolk accent. He was one of the few people who addressed the vicar by his Christian name. "Ow's it 'anging then?'

The vicar knew Bernie was teasing him by being a bit cheeky, but he didn't mind.

'Just fine, thank you,' said the vicar, 'and how's Molly?'

Molly was Bernie's wife. Like Bernie, she was also built on the generous side of mountainous. But she wasn't fat – she worked too hard for that – just big.

'She's a'reet, Cliff. Busy up at t' farm, oi reckons.'

'Well, give her my best, won't you?'

'Roight you are, Cliff. Oi sees you laters.'

As the vicar turned round from speaking to Bernie, he noticed a young lady at the other end of the churchyard, seemingly chatting to the world in general, for no one else appeared to be there. Being curious, the vicar made his way over to investigate. As he got nearer, he could see that the lady in question was Cecilia Dawson. She was an attractive young woman, with blonde shoulder-length hair and startling blue eyes. The vicar knew she worked in Holt as an accountant's secretary. She was a clever and resourceful girl, but also shy and demure. What he couldn't understand was why she was talking to herself in the churchyard. And then he heard it. He thought he could hear another voice. A man's voice. But no one was there. *Odd*, thought the vicar. He was almost behind her, so he decided to make his presence known by giving a gentle cough.

Cecilia gave a sharp intake of breath and spun round in surprise to face the vicar. At the same time, a young man's head popped up from behind one of the churchyard's nearby gravestones. He'd obviously been sitting with his back leaning against the gravestone and the vicar had not been able to see him. Cecilia had clearly not been talking to herself after all.

'I do apologise,' said the vicar. 'I didn't mean to disturb you.'

Cecilia blushed and murmured, 'That's quite all right. You just made me jump.'

The young man looked alarmed and was fidgeting about awkwardly.

Cecilia continued, 'This is Michael – a friend of mine.'

The vicar looked at Michael and enquired, 'Ah, you must be Cynthia's son?'

Michael looked positively panic-stricken. 'You won't tell her, will you?' he jabbered. 'She doesn't like me being over here.'

'Over here?' queried the vicar.

'In East Barton,' Michael explained.

The vicar was still puzzled. 'Why ever not?'

Cecilia leant over and grasped the vicar's hand. 'Please, Vicar,' she begged. 'Please promise not to tell anyone.'

'Well, of course, my dear,' he said, patting her hand, 'as you wish. Mum's the word.'

'Mum?' said Michael, looking worried.

'No, no,' explained the vicar, 'it's just an expression.'

Michael breathed a sigh of relief. Then, he and Cecilia scuttled away in opposite directions, taking great care not to be seen.

The vicar shook his head and wondered what on earth that was all about. The strange episode had concerned him somewhat, but he put it to the back of his mind and once again mounted his old bicycle. *What an odd day this is turning out to be*, he thought.

It was about to get odder.

He didn't have to go far. Just a few houses further along stood the vicarage. A fine double-fronted Georgian house, with a fabulous array of pink, magenta and white clematis climbing over the front aspect, all the way to the roof line.

Not many of the clergy lived in vicarages anymore since most of the properties had been flogged off years ago to prop up the church coffers. Reverend Rose, for example, lived in a far more modest cottage, in nearby Little Walsingham. The church provided it gratis, so he wasn't complaining.

The inhabitant of this vicarage, however, was Brigadier Gerald Faraday, who was unnecessarily trimming the already perfect clematis with a pair of miniature shears. He was in his mid-sixties, of medium height, with thinning gingery hair either side of his bald pate and a thick, bristling moustache. He had a ruddy,

11

choleric, chubby face, watery blue eyes and was well known to have an extremely short and fierce temper. He'd been in the army all his life since graduating from Sandhurst and gaining his commission as an officer. The military life had suited him well. He'd shouted his orders and men had jumped into action and carried them out. He was a confirmed bachelor, so the scarcity of women during his career had not bothered him in the least. Now retired, he often struggled to fit in with civilian life, as the military style was so ingrained in him.

Having spied the approaching vicar, the brigadier stopped what he was doing, rested his shears on his rather portly stomach and turned to greet him.

'Morning, Rose,' he bellowed. He always called men by their surname – another legacy from his army days. 'Doing the rounds, I see – what!'

'I was—' began the vicar but was immediately interrupted.

'Don't suppose you've seen that Cecilia girl around, have you? Promised my sister I'd keep an eye on her, y'see.'

The vicar thought for a moment and put two and two together. 'I didn't know Cecilia was your niece. I just—'

'Of course she's me damned niece, man. Wouldn't be asking otherwise. Well?'

'Well… what?'

'Have you seen her, man?' boomed the brigadier, who seemed to be getting a little irate.

'Oh, no. No, I haven't seen her,' said the vicar, forced into telling his second lie of the day.

'Well, if you do, you can tell her to stay away from that Smythe boy. I've seen her canoodling with him. He's a rum one and no mistake – what!'

'I really couldn't—' he started to reply but was cut off for the third time.

'I suppose you've been over to the West this morning then?'

'West Barton? Yes, I've just—'

'And what have they all been up to then, eh? The blaggards!'

'I'm not sure I'm with you, Gerald,' said the vicar, although he knew very well what the brigadier was getting at. It was no secret that the brigadier was chair of the EBBKVC and this was his unsubtle way of trying to dig for information.

'Hah! Keeping shtum, are you? Well, not to worry, we have our ways of finding these things out, you know,' said the brigadier, tapping his nose conspiratorially with his shears and nearly poking his eye out in the process. Although he narrowly avoided blinding himself, he did accidentally cut himself.

'Confounded things!' he yelled as he threw the shears to the ground and then clutched his face dramatically. He lowered his hands slowly. 'Blood!' he yelped. The vicar could see a tiny smear of red on his hands that had come from a minuscule nick above the brigadier's nose. 'I'm wounded!' he wailed.

As the brigadier began ranting, railing and haranguing the world in general, the vicar took the opportunity to disappear and left him to it.

He rode out of the village to continue on his way and mulled over all the exchanges that had occurred that morning. He concluded that West and East Barton were particularly eccentric and peculiar places, and swore to himself that he wasn't going to get involved in this blighted Best Kept Village Competition – if he could possibly help it.

2.

It was 7pm on the following Friday evening and The Barton Arms had been open for an hour and a half. Keith was on duty and was looking particularly sullen as he surveyed the room. The pub was almost deserted. Only old Bill Rolls was propping up the bar. He usually stopped in for a pint before heading back home for his supper. He still lived up at the farm with Bernie and Molly. Bill had lost his beloved wife, Judy, some years ago. Since her passing, he'd let Bernie and Molly live in the main farmhouse and he'd moved into the converted barn in the farmyard, which served very nicely as a comfortable annexe.

'Another pint, Bill?' asked Keith, as Bill drained the last few dregs from his glass.

'Nah, I'm roight, thaanks,' he said. 'I'd better be gettin' meself baack home. Oi see ye tomorra though.'

He plonked his pint glass back on the bar, stood up and unsteadily made his way out to the car park. It wasn't the beer that made him unsteady. He was nearly ninety years old and his aged limbs were giving him gyp. He climbed into his battered estate car and slowly drove off towards East Barton.

Back in the pub, Keith sighed, picked up the empty beer glass and began to wash it up in the sink. It wasn't worth using the dishwasher – there wasn't ever enough to put in it. *We can't carry on like this*, he thought, *or we'll soon be bust*. Since buying the pub and moving into the area, he'd become aware that there was some sort of feud going on between West and East Barton. All over some daft competition, apparently. But he'd noticed a worrying trend; if anyone from East Barton was in the pub, then invariably no one from West Barton would come in. And vice versa. It was not good for business. It was no wonder they'd bought the pub for such a good price. He was beginning to see why.

Still, they did have a booking tonight for the private dining room at 7:30pm. Jenny was busy in the kitchen preparing for it. The booking was in the name of Barrington-Smyth and was for four people.

As Keith placed the glass back on the rack, the front door of the pub opened gently and a small sour-faced lady, entirely clad in tartan, walked briskly up to the bar. Keith had never seen her before.

'Good evening, madam,' he greeted her. 'What can I get for you?'

'A dry sherry, if you please,' Ethel brusquely replied. 'Just to take the chill off my old bones, you understand.'

Keith looked puzzled. It was an unseasonably warm

spring this year. It had reached 25°C in the midday sun, and the nights were balmy and warm, too. What chill she was referring to, he had no idea. He just shrugged and nodded.

As Keith turned away to pour the sherry, Ethel took the opportunity to survey the pub. She did not feel at all comfortable in public bars, especially on her own. She frowned upon pubs and bars in general, seeing them as dens of iniquity, and would certainly not be here if it wasn't for Brigadier Faraday's insistence.

The brigadier had finally found Cecilia and challenged her about her friendship with Michael, insisting that it stop at once. In the ensuing argument, Cecilia had let slip that Michael had told her his mother and some 'friends' from West Barton were going for a meal at the pub tonight. The brigadier had correctly surmised that this was actually a meeting of the WBBKVC and the sneaky fiends were trying to do it in private. These meetings were usually held in the respective village halls, where anyone was free to attend.

The brigadier had rung round the members of his own committee and, between them, they'd hatched a plan to send Ethel up to the pub to eavesdrop on them. The brigadier had given her a crisp £20 note from the EBBKVC petty cash tin to cover her expenses. Ethel had raised an eyebrow at the obvious misappropriation of committee funds, but had quickly whisked the money into her voluminous tartan handbag regardless.

'That will be £5, please,' said Keith, sliding the sherry glass across the bar to her.

After much protracted rummaging in her bag, Ethel produced the £20 note and reluctantly placed it into Keith's waiting hand. As he went to the till to ring it in, he thought he heard her muttering something about 'daylight robbery', but he smiled sweetly and handed her back her change.

She whipped it smartly back into the depths of her bag and, snapping it shut, she gave Keith a hurt look as if to suggest she'd just been brutally mugged. Clutching the sherry, she sidled off to a side part of the pub, known as The Snug. As luck would have it, The Snug was decorated and furnished in a Highland style. She settled herself onto the huge sofa, blending in nicely with the Harris Tweed upholstery – and was perfectly camouflaged. She took a sip of her sherry, which barely wet her lips. Being of a thrifty nature, she could make a single sherry last all night. She leaned back into the sofa and waited.

Back at the bar, Keith was just lamenting the fact that one pint of beer and a small sherry were hardly likely to keep the business afloat when the front door opened again.

Cynthia Barrington-Smythe, Vincent Kleeb and Dr Maryam Jahan entered the pub and slowly made their way to the bar. They'd all arrived in one car. Vincent had offered a lift to all members of the committee in one of his luxurious processional limos. All but Richard Braithwaite had accepted the invitation. Richard had bluntly told them that he wouldn't be seen dead in one of those funeral cars and – oblivious to the irony of his remark – insisted on driving separately in his 4x4.

'Good evening, all,' said Keith, 'and welcome to The Barton Arms.'

'Good evening,' replied Cynthia, 'we have a table booked at 7:30pm in the private dining room.'

'Ah, yes. The Barrington-Smythe party?'

'That is correct.'

'And would you like a drink in the bar before you go through?'

'We'll order drinks and take them through with us, if that's all right with you.'

'Certainly, certainly,' said Keith. 'Now, what can I get you?'

As they ordered their drinks, they chatted amiably among themselves. Ethel, out of sight around the corner, was craning her neck to try and hear the conversation.

'Richard's a bit late,' commented Maryam.

'Typical of him,' sneered Vincent, who was still in a snit with him over the rude rebuke of his offer of a lift.

The drinks were ready and Keith had put them on a tray. 'Shall I take them through for you?' he asked.

'Most kind,' said Maryam.

'This way, then,' he said and he led them through the bar to the private dining room, which was adjacent to The Snug. They took their places at the dining table and Keith placed the drinks down before them, then passed them the menu to peruse.

As he left the dining room and passed back into the bar, a screeching of brakes and sliding of gravel could be heard from the car park, which marked the tardy arrival of Lord Braithwaite.

Moments later, the front door flew open with a bang and in strutted Richard, reeking of cologne and dressed in his finest country attire. He wore shiny brown brogues, yellow corduroy trousers and a farmer-style checked shirt. A tweed sports jacket, emblazoned with his own crest of arms, and a flat cap embroidered with a logo of two crossed shotguns finished the ensemble.

'Barkeep!' he shouted from the doorway. 'A whisky, please, and make it a double.' He strode up to the bar, hand outstretched. 'I'm Richard Braithwaite,' he said, as if he were some sort of A-list celebrity, and shook Keith's hand vigorously.

'I'm Keith Atkins – the new *landlord*,' said Keith, who was a bit peeved at being called barkeep. 'Is the house whisky all right?'

'Good God, no – can't stomach that muck. Always malt whisky for me. Little bit of ice and a splash of water.'

'Very good, sir,' said Keith and poured him the whisky.

'And how's business?' enquired Richard.

'It's a little quiet, to be honest.'

'Yes, I can see that,' said Richard, looking round the bar. 'Well, if you want my advice, what you need is to be more proactive, man! Grab the bull by the horns! *Carpe diem* and all that. That's what I'd do. Cheers!' He knocked the whisky straight back. 'I'll have another one of those, please. Make it a double this time.'

'That was a double, sir,' said Keith.

'Oh, well, if you say so. Barely wet the glass.'

Keith was a calm and patient man, but was starting to get mightily irritated by this arrogant buffoon. 'Your friends are waiting for you in the private dining room, sir. I'll bring your drink through, if you like,' he offered.

'Oh, very well. Here goes then!' He pretended to straighten his tie and, with a shout of 'Tally-ho!', lurched off towards the dining room, much to Keith's great relief.

'Thanks for the advice, by the way,' said Keith sarcastically, but Richard didn't hear. Even if he had, it would have been lost on him. He genuinely thought he'd been insightful and useful.

Richard reached the private dining room and headed inside.

'Ah, Richard, here you are at last,' said Cynthia. 'Do sit down and we can get on with business. We need to discuss exactly what we are doing for the first day of judging.'

The door to the dining room had been left open and Ethel could hear every word from her secret spot in The Snug. What passed for a smile appeared on her face.

But just then, Keith reappeared with Richard's second whisky and went into the dining room to give it to him. He also had a pad in hand ready to take the food order. He closed the door behind him and Ethel could no longer hear the conversation.

'Darn it!' she mumbled to herself. Now what was she going to do? She thought for a moment and then a flash of inspiration dawned across her face. She reached for her huge tartan handbag, opened it and began rummaging inside. She produced various items from her bag and placed them on a nearby table. The variety and quantity of items emerging from her bag would have impressed *Mary Poppins*. So far, there were some spectacles, a purse, a hairbrush, lipstick, perfume, a can of baked beans (for survival in the event of nuclear war), a compact mirror, her house keys and a box of tissues. Finally, she located what she was searching for and triumphantly pulled out an ear trumpet. Ethel was a little hard of hearing, but refused to wear hearing aids, relying instead on this antiquated invention. She hastily shoved all of the other items back in her bag and held the ear trumpet up to the wall. She placed the funnelled end in her own ear and listened intently, her face screwed up in concentration.

She couldn't hear a thing. *Drat*, she thought, and decided it was time to call it a day. She slipped out of the back door of the pub and walked home. It would seem the slight flaw in the EBBKVC's otherwise meticulously cunning plan was in sending someone who was as deaf as a post on an eavesdropping operation.

Inside the dining room, Keith was hovering by the table, waiting to take the group's food order and having to endure listening to a lengthy discussion about flower displays.

Cynthia, as ever, was insisting that her tulip display should be the main feature for the first day of judging. This year, she had produced a multicoloured tulip display, which she was calling "Tutti Frutti". She told the others that their duties were to ensure that the village was clean and tidy, the grass was cut, hedges trimmed and so on and so forth.

Keith noted that none of them argued with her, not even his lordship. Keith finally managed to take the order. As he exited the dining room, he popped his head round the corner to check on The Snug. The strange Scottish lady had disappeared, along with the sherry. Just the empty glass remained, which he picked up and took back to the bar with him.

When Keith went back to serve the wine, the group were still talking about flower displays or some such tripe, only this time they were trying to guess what East Barton were going to do. They kept mentioning the brigadier's clematis – whatever that meant.

The rest of the evening passed by in a similar vein. Jenny had excelled herself in the kitchen, providing a top-notch meal, and their guests were very happy and contented. One, in particular, was very merry. Richard had drunk rather too much and as the party rose to leave, he had a discernible wobble.

'I think, Richard,' said Cynthia, adopting a stern tone, 'that you'd better let Vincent drive you home with the rest of us.'

Vincent rolled his eyes and tutted.

Richard fixed her with a bleary gaze. 'I am pershectly capable of getting myshelf home, shank you, Missus Badminton-Smile.'

'Barrington-Smyth,' corrected Cynthia, 'and you most certainly are not. You will come with us this instant.'

Richard didn't argue further. Vincent and Maryam grabbed an arm each and assisted him out of the pub. They bade Keith farewell on the way out and asked if it was all right if Richard's car could be picked up in the morning. Keith nodded that it was no problem.

They drove Richard home first. His staff were waiting for him under the grand entrance portico of Barton Hall. As they watched the big black limo come to a halt and saw the inert body of Lord Braithwaite sprawled out in the back, they wondered if they might have lost their employer in a tragic accident. But unfortunately, it turned out he was only dead drunk.

*

Back at the pub, all was quiet again. Keith went to the kitchen to help Jenny with washing the dishes. He told her what they'd been talking about all evening and she found it quite interesting. Not the flowers, particularly, but the level of obsession they had regarding the competition. *She has a point there*, thought Keith.

While Jenny slipped off upstairs to bed, Keith went off to do his rounds and lock up for the night.

3.

'Order! Order! Settle down!' hollered the brigadier, as he strode importantly into the silent and largely empty village hall. 'I hereby call to order the first meeting of the East Barton Best Kept Village Committee – Brigadier Gerald Faraday presiding.'

The brigadier did like his formalities.

'In attendance at the village hall are…' he continued, 'Cecilia Dawson.'

'Here!' piped up Cecilia. She was secretary of the committee and had been given the task of taking the minutes.

'Ethel McKinley.'

'What?' said Ethel.

'Are you here?'

'What do you mean, am I here?'

'For the register, Ethel, are you here?'

'Oh, I see. Aye, then. I'm here.'

'Bernard Rolls.'

'Is this really necessary?' complained Bernie.

'Bernard Rolls ' repeated the brigadier, with just a hint of tetchiness.

'Oh, all roight,' said Bernie, with a sigh, 'I'm 'ere, too.'

'Absentees?'

'If there were any, they wouldn't be 'ere to say so, would they?' said Bernie with a slight smirk.

The brigadier ignored him and continued with his bumptious address. 'Good morning, team. I hope you're all fighting fit on this fine day. Let's get straight down to business.' He'd taken the liberty of bringing his swagger stick with him, which he was now slapping into his hand for dramatic effect. 'The first judging day of the competition, as we're all aware, is tomorrow.'

The first leg of the Best Kept Village Competition was always held in spring. The judges were looking for villages that, in general, were well maintained, clean and tidy, and for there to be one individual display. This normally consisted of one property to be picked out from their respective villages and judged on the quality and beauty of its display.

'Now, we're all in agreement that the initial day will feature my clematis, are we not?' said the brigadier, tucking the swagger stick under his arm in a military fashion.

They all murmured their agreement.

'Very well. And I'm sure you've all been busy looking after your own responsibilities regarding the competition?' he enquired, giving them a beady eye.

They murmured agreement again.

'I'm sure you won't let me down.' He beamed at them in what he thought was a Churchillian-style rousing manner. 'We do want everything to be shipshape and Bristol fashion – what.'

They all nodded enthusiastically.

'Now,' he said, narrowing his eyes conspiratorially, 'what we really need to know is what the enemy are up to, eh. The swines!'

There was an audible gasp from Cecilia. 'The enemy? Swines?' she queried, looking appalled. 'Don't you mean the other competitors?'

The brigadier was a little taken aback by this mutinous interruption to his carefully rehearsed speech. As he mulled it over, twiddling his moustache as if in deep thought, he finally conceded. 'Oh, well, yes,' he said sheepishly, 'I suppose you'd better strike that from the record. Please change that to read "competitors".'

Cecilia made the necessary correction in her notepad.

The brigadier returned to his theme. 'Ethel, I believe, has some important intelligence for us in this regard. Isn't that right, Ethel?' he prompted.

'Oh, yes, I most certainly do,' said Ethel, folding her arms and looking smug.

'Right, Ethel, you have the chair,' said the brigadier.

'I've already got one,' she said, looking round confused.

'No, no, I mean you can now tell us all what you've found out,' explained the brigadier, looking exasperated.

'Oh,' she said, 'right you are.'

She rose to her feet and, warming to her subject, she began her tale. 'Well, there they all were. The West Barton lot. Up at the pub,' she said distastefully. 'In the bar. And in the restaurant. Drinking and eating. Talking and laughing. And *carrying on!*' She sat down again with a look of abject shock and horror on her face. 'I've never seen the likes of it!' she added.

The other committee members looked at each other quizzically, with the mutual feeling that they'd all perhaps turned two pages at once.

'Well said, Ethel!' chipped in Bernie for good measure, though he had no idea what she was on about.

The brigadier was agog. Either Ethel had something red-hot up her sleeve, he concluded, or she was as mad as a hatter wrestling a box of frogs off a March hare. As he studied her face for a further reaction, he was leaning towards the latter.

'Then what happened?' he ventured.

'You want *more*?' said Ethel, looking surprised.

'But Ethel,' said Cecilia, trying to be the voice of reason, 'going to the pub for a drink and a meal isn't a crime and…'

'It's disgraceful!' insisted Ethel, giving Cecilia a filthy look. Ethel's puritanical side knew no bounds. She made Mary Whitehouse look like a lascivious libertine.

'But did you find out anything about the competition?' asked the brigadier, who was still desperately hoping there was going to be some point to this conversation.

'Oh no, not really, dear,' said Ethel.

The brigadier was starting to regret splashing out £20 of committee funds on this clearly dotty old pensioner.

'But everyone knows Cynthia will be doing her tulip display again,' she stated matter-of-factly.

Oh, do they now? thought the brigadier. He'd suspected as much and now it was confirmed. Well then, he'd just have to make sure his clematis display outshone her tulips.

Half an hour later, the meeting wound up. A few folks from the village had wondered in about halfway through, hoping to cadge some free tea and biscuits, but, other than that, there was nothing more of note to report.

That afternoon, both Bartons were hives of activity. The inhabitants of the two villages were busy bustling around, tidying, mowing, painting, weeding, watering and pruning. Once everyone was satisfied that perfection had been attained, they retired early for the evening, in readiness for the big day. As night drew in, all was quiet.

4.

It was 2am in the middle of the night. The sky was clear and the stars were shining brightly. The moon was almost full and it was possible to see quite well just by the moonlight. There was no street lighting in the Bartons. They were part of an environmentally friendly trend known as "Dark-Skies villages". The idea being to go back to nature and to prevent light pollution. It also earned you a bonus point from the judges of the Best Kept Village Competition.

At that moment, a dark figure in the shadows was also thinking that the lack of light was a bonus.

The figure was clad all in black, including a balaclava which covered the face and head with only the eyes and mouth showing. The Lincoln-green gardening gloves were the only things that detracted from the otherwise invisible prowler. One of the gloved hands was clutching a pair of newly sharpened secateurs.

It approached the cottage belonging to Cynthia

Barrington-Smythe and neatly hopped over her white picket fence into her stunning garden. The heads of her tulips could be clearly seen, swaying slightly in the gentle breeze. Moments later, a quiet snip, snip, snipping sound could be heard and the heads of her magnificent tulips fluttered gently to the ground.

Ten minutes later, the figure hopped back over the fence and vanished once again into the shadows. Every single one of the tulips had been beheaded.

Not long after, another mysterious figure, identically dressed in black but with navy-blue gardening gloves, was lurking by the brigadier's stone front wall. One gloved hand was holding a bottle containing an insipid-looking liquid. The figure vaulted the wall and disappeared momentarily into the undergrowth. It reappeared a few seconds later at the side of the brigadier's house and made its way slowly round the corner to where the clematis was planted along the front of the property. A faint pop could be heard as the bottle was opened. The figure crawled along the entire length of the house, pouring the lethal liquid into each and every root system of the clematis. A hissing noise could be heard every time the liquid was poured, followed by a potent acrid whiff.

Once the job was done, the figure crawled back over the wall and slinked off into the darkness.

5.

The first day of the competition had finally come around. The judges had arrived promptly at 9am in all competing villages in the district. The weather was staying fine – a little overcast, but no rain forecast. In West Barton, the judge was making her rounds, clipboard in hand, and going through the checklist for the first leg of the competition. She was very impressed so far with what she had seen. The village was immaculate and stunningly beautiful. All categories thus far had scored a resounding ten out of ten. All that remained to be judged was the individual property display. A small throng, consisting of judge, committee members and hangers-on, were making their way to Cynthia Barrington-Smythe's pretty cottage where they were to be enthralled with her "Tutti Frutti" tulip display. Richard, Maryam and Vincent were a bit surprised Cynthia had not joined them at the very beginning for the procession round the village, but had assumed she was making some last-minute improvements.

As they neared her cottage, they could see Cynthia standing stock-still in her garden. Nearer still, they could see that her face was set like a rock, her mouth taut and her thin lips clenched tightly together. Her eyes were glaring icily at her garden. She was obviously livid with anger. As the small throng reached her side, they all felt the same sensation that the temperature had suddenly dropped several degrees. Following her gaze, the cause of her anger became immediately apparent. Instead of a stunning array of tulips, there was now only a garden full of stalks and, on the ground, a wilting carpet of browning tulip heads.

'Well, this won't do at all,' said the judge sniffily. 'I can only award one point – for *trying*. And that's all, I'm afraid.'

Cynthia's head shot round and she fixed the judge with a look of such sheer loathing that the poor lady visibly reeled back in fear. Cynthia drew a long breath and was about to give the judge a verbal savaging so severe that she'd never want to step foot in West Barton again, when she managed, with great restraint, to control herself.

Between gritted teeth, she said, 'I think it is obvious that foul play has been at work here. My tulip display was in full blossom yesterday and this...' she said, pointing at her ruined garden, 'is the work of a vandal.' *And*, she mused, *I've got a very clear idea who it might be.*

'I'm calling the police,' she snapped. 'Everyone out of my garden. Now!'

The small throng were only too happy to oblige. They had scarce seen Cynthia in such a temper and no one wanted to be on the receiving end of her barbed tongue. They legged it.

Meanwhile, in East Barton, a similar throng was trailing round the village, following in the footsteps of their judge, who was also greatly impressed with what he was seeing. The village looked gorgeous and was dazzlingly clean and neat. Straight tens across the board had been scored. Only the brigadier's clematis display remained. Cecilia, Bernie and Ethel were all beaming with pride as they headed towards the vicarage.

But then the tranquillity of the moment was rudely shattered by a ferocious yelling…

'*What the bloody blue blazes* !!' could be heard being bellowed across the village. It was the brigadier and he didn't sound at all happy.

Goodness me, thought Ethel. *What on earth is Gerald doing, shouting such profanities?* In all her days, she'd never heard such foul language. And in front of the judge, too!

As they rushed over to the vicarage to see what the commotion was all about, they could see the brigadier desperately trying to hold his clematis onto the front of his house – but to no avail. The clematis was discolouring and peeling off the wall in huge clumps.

On seeing the sorry spectacle, the judge shook his head and scored it a measly one out of ten on his clipboard.

'Whatever has happened?' asked Cecilia, looking shocked.

'Some damned bounder has poisoned my clematis! That's what's bloody well happened!' ranted the brigadier, whose face was turning red with fury. The ground all around the base of the clematis was scorched and the roots were still smoking. 'It's sabotage, I tell you!' he fumed, and then paused in thought at his own words. As the penny dropped into his mind, he continued, 'Yes, and it dashed well is sabotage, as well. And I know exactly who's responsible!' He turned to Cecilia and shouted, 'I want the law here, right now!'

'Yes, Uncle,' said Cecilia as she rushed into the house to make the call.

6.

Sergeant Dale Richards was sat in the canteen at Fakenham Police Station, enjoying a cup of tea and a custard cream. He'd just finished his morning rounds and was on a twenty-minute break. Dale was a Yorkshireman, born and bred in Barnsley. His father, Oswald, was of the Windrush generation and had emigrated from Jamaica in 1955, and joined the Barnsley Constabulary shortly after. The Richards were coppers through and through. Dale's grandfather had been a policeman in Kingston and his father before him. It was in the blood. Dale, like his father, had cut his teeth in Barnsley, but he'd then gone on to policing in the bigger city of Sheffield. And there, he'd seen it all. Drugs, prostitution, hooliganism, burglaries, racism, fraud, gang wars and even murder. He'd had an interesting and fulfilling career. Sometimes, it had been hard. Often, it had been dangerous. Now he was approaching retirement age and he'd had enough excitement for one life. He'd requested to be reposted somewhere a little quieter for him to wind down his last few years before packing in policing for good. He and his wife, Linda, had enjoyed holidays in Norfolk over the years, so when the chance came up of a relocation to the county, he'd jumped at it.

The handheld radio strapped to his belt crackled to life. 'Hiya!' came the unmistakeably boyish voice of Constable Josh Crowther. 'Are you there, Sarge?' Josh was a new recruit, currently working the front desk. He was from Kings Lynn but had recently moved to Fakenham with his partner, Robin. To say Josh was camp would be somewhat of an understatement. He made Larry Grayson look butch.

'I've told you before, PC Crowther. You need to use the proper police-approved etiquette when communicating by radio.'

'Sorry, Sarge,' said Josh, pretending to sound chastised. He tried again. 'Come in, Sergeant Richards. Are you there? I've got an urgent call for you.'

'Aye, I'm here, lad,' said Dale. 'Roger that.'

'I beg your pardon?' said Josh, trying not to giggle.

'It means – *Yes, I understand.* Now, would you kindly tell me what you want?'

'Roger!' said Josh, endowing the word with ulterior meaning. 'Well, I've got an odd one for you here, Sarge. Two reports of vandalism. One call from West Barton, then, about five minutes later, we got another from East Barton.'

'Nothing odd there, son,' said Dale. 'Probably some

youths out joyriding through the villages. Tell them I'm on my way.'

'Roger,' said Josh again, extracting a little more sass before signing off.

Dale was already regretting teaching him the phrase. He raised his eyes to the heavens, finished his tea and biscuit, grabbed his helmet and went out to the car park. He fired up his Ford Mondeo squad car, switched on the flashing lights and siren, and drove off towards the Bartons.

*

Cynthia was sat at her kitchen table with the other members of the committee, who were trying, unsuccessfully, to console her. They were discussing who exactly could have done such a thing and the answer was always the same. The only ones who had a motive for this atrocity were the East Barton Best Kept Village Committee. It was obvious. Talk was progressing as to which one of them actually did it, when they heard the sound of the approaching siren. They all stood and walked out of the house as the police car came to a halt outside. The siren and lights were switched off and Dale got out of the car. He was a tall, well-built man and he'd kept himself fit over the years. He was just starting to lose some of the muscle tone and had gained a few pounds about his midriff, but he still presented a formidable figure. As it was a warm day, he'd discarded his jacket and was in his shirt sleeves and tie. He donned his helmet, pulled the strap under his chin and walked over to the group of people assembled by the front gate.

'Good afternoon,' he greeted them, 'my name is Sergeant Richards. I'll be dealing with this case.' He pulled a notepad and pen from his pocket and started to read from it. 'At 11:15am today, we had a report of a disturbance—'

'A disturbance! Huh!' interrupted Cynthia. 'I should say it's a lot more serious than that.'

'Hear! Hear!' piped up Richard, trying to affect a stern expression.

Dale gave him the once-over and then turned back to Cynthia. 'And your name, madam?'

'Cynthia Barrington-Smythe,' she snapped.

'Ah, yes. And you are the owner of the property?'

'I am.'

'Would you like to describe to me exactly what has happened?'

'I'll do more than that. I will show you,' she said, with a sorrowful tone to her voice.

She led the policeman through the gate and into her garden. With a hand shaking with emotion, she gesticulated towards her garden and then averted her eyes as if it were too painful to countenance the horror again.

Dale looked into her garden and could see that someone had made a right royal mess of her flowers. *Good grief, though*, he thought, *if that's all she's moaning on about. The things I get called out for...*

'Terrible,' he said, trying to be sympathetic.

'Yes,' she whispered in anguish, 'all decapitated!'

'Indeed,' he nodded.

'Dead!' She sighed. 'All dead!'

'Aye. No doubt about it,' he said.

'Is that *all* you have to say about it, sergeant?' she asked huffily, dabbing at her eyes with a handkerchief.

Sergeant Richards didn't get her drift. He gave her question some thought and drawing on his years of experience dealing with the eccentric British middle classes, he finally thought he had an inkling what she might be expecting from him. He fished in his pocket and produced a black armband, which he wrapped around his left arm. With great deference, he removed his helmet and bowed his head.

'On behalf of myself and the Norfolk Constabulary, I would like to extend our deepest condolences for your loss at this difficult time and—'

'That is *not* what I meant,' said Cynthia sniffily. She rolled her eyes. 'What I meant was… what are you going to *do* about it?'

'Oh, right,' said Dale. Realising he'd been barking up the wrong tree, he hastily removed the armband and donned his helmet again.

'Well?' asked Cynthia.

'Well,' said Dale, regaining his composure, 'can you think of anyone who might bear you a grudge?'

'Yes, she can,' cut in Richard. '*Captain Mainwaring*, for one.'

'And the rest of *Dad's Army*,' sniped Vincent.

Dale looked puzzled.

'They mean Brigadier Faraday and his committee from East Barton,' explained Maryam. 'They are our rivals in the competition, you see.'

'Competition? What competition?' asked Dale, making notes in his pad.

'Why, the Best Kept Village Competition, of course,' said Cynthia.

'I see,' said Dale.

'That's why her tulip display has been vandalised,' added Vincent. 'It's bound to have been them.'

'Well, let's not jump to conclusions,' advised Dale.

'Nonsense,' chided Cynthia, 'it must be them. I suggest you get straight over there and arrest them all right away.'

Sergeant Richards disliked being told how to do his job. He rounded on Cynthia. 'For your information, I am already due to pay them a visit straight after we have concluded here. You see, we have received a complaint of vandalism from them also.'

Cynthia looked at him, dumbfounded.

That stole her thunder, thought Dale.

'Right then,' he said, 'do any of you have anything further to add?'

They all looked at him blankly.

'In that case, I'll be on my way. You may rest assured I will be bringing the matter up with this Brigadier Faraday,' said Dale, as he turned his back on them and headed back to the squad car.

He fired up the Mondeo and headed off down the

road to West Barton. Passing The Barton Arms along the way, he made a mental note to himself that he must pop in and introduce himself to the new owners sometime soon. He drove into West Barton, past the village green and the church, and pulled up alongside the stone wall of the vicarage. As he got out of the car, he saw a red-faced man angrily raking up what looked like piles of rancid weeds outside the front of the house. There were three others loitering nearby, presumably the other committee members.

'Good day, all,' he greeted them.

The red-faced man looked up from his raking. 'Good?' barked the brigadier. 'There's been nothing bloody good about it!' He was still in a foul mood. The others had tried to calm him down over the last few hours, but had just earned themselves a mouthful of abuse for their efforts. 'And what time do you call this? We rang for the police hours ago!' he continued his raging.

Dale wasn't used to being addressed like this and was about to take umbrage with the man, when Bernie thought it wise to intervene. He walked over to Dale and extended a massive paw of a hand. 'Thank ye for comin' over so quick. Oi'm Bernie. Bernie Rolls.' He cupped his hand round his mouth and whispered to Dale, 'Don't mind 'im. He's 'ad a bad day.'

'I'm Sergeant Richards,' said Dale, shaking Bernie's hand. 'I'm here to investigate the incident.'

'*Sabotage*!' boomed the brigadier. 'Sabotage is what it was! No incident. No accident. Downright dastardly *sabotage*! Just look at my clematis.'

So that's what it was, thought Dale. He had to admit it looked in a pretty sorry state. It was still falling off the wall in random clumps.

'Forty years old that clematis was,' lamented the brigadier, 'and some swine has gone and poisoned it. Sabotage, I tell you.'

Dale thought he'd strike while the iron was hot. 'I have just been to West Barton,' he informed them, 'where a similar act of vandalism has been carried out to the garden of a Mrs Barrington-Smythe.'

This information caused them all to raise an eyebrow.

'Mrs Barrington-Smythe and her colleagues,' continued Dale, 'were under the distinct impression that your committee may have had something to do with it.'

'Oh! That's what the *Wicked Witch of the West* thinks, is it?' bawled the brigadier, getting fired up again. 'Well, I think it was her or one of her rotten minions that wrecked my sodding clematis! I'll have their guts for garters!' His face was going a worrying shade of purple.

'Now, let's just keep calm,' said Cecilia, trying to sooth the situation.

'*I am perfectly bloody calm!*' roared the brigadier, contradicting himself. 'I just want to get the bugger responsible!'

'Gerald!' scolded Ethel. 'Will you kindly refrain from such crude expletives.'

The brigadier turned to stare goggle-eyed at Ethel, but seeing the look of offended piousness in her eyes, he faltered and muttered an apology, 'I'm sorry, my dear, but it gets my goat!'

'Now, everyone listen to me,' said Dale sternly. He'd just about had enough of this nonsense. 'I'm aware of the competition going on at the moment and the rivalry between you and West Barton. That's very clear. Now, I don't know exactly what's been going on, but I strongly suggest that you all just try and get along. It's only a competition at the end of the day. It's supposed to be fun.'

'You mean you're not going to sort that lot out?' asked the brigadier with surprise.

'I have no evidence, sir. Just hearsay. You must understand there's little I can do in that regard. However, what I do propose doing is going back to the station and I'm going to have a formal letter typed up – to be sent to both West and East Barton committees – warning against any further transgressions upon penalty of the law. And I do suggest you all take heed.'

They all nodded their assent and that was that.

Dale was pleased with how he'd dealt with the situation. For one, he'd managed to shut the fiery-tempered brigadier up, and for two, he'd put the frosty Mrs Barrington-Smythe in her place. Not a bad day's work.

He made his way back to the squad car and settled himself behind the wheel of the Mondeo. *God's teeth*, he thought. Some of the things people got het up about really did baffle him. He sighed and slowly drove back to the police station – and the real world.

7.

As spring turned into summer, the next leg of the competition was fast approaching. Despite Sergeant Richards' attempt to keep the peace between the two villages, tensions had continued to simmer. Speculation and intrigue had grown following the incidents of vandalism during the first leg of the competition. No one could quite believe what had taken place, and gossip and suspicions were running high as to who had carried out the sordid deeds. Neither committee had any real clue as to who had done what. While each committee had been appalled at the vandalism they had sustained, each was also secretly pleased that someone had had the nerve to retaliate on their behalf.

Cecilia and Michael's relationship had been put under severe sanctions. Cynthia had forbidden Michael to see Cecilia. She was damned if she was going to have her son in cahoots with the niece of *Colonel Blimp*. And, in turn, the brigadier had made it very clear to Cecilia that he didn't want her to have anything to do with the son of the *Ice Queen*. Cecilia and Michael were not to be so easily swayed, however, and had been having secret trysts in the churchyards of both villages. More than once, Reverend Rose had caught them together and had had to turn a blind eye.

Keith and Jenny were still battling on at the pub. The increased tensions and rivalry between the Bartons were not helping their business. The pub was as quiet as ever. The only new customer they'd picked up was the local policeman, Dale Richards, who'd dropped in one day to say hello. He and Keith had got on well, and now Dale came in regularly of an evening. He'd even been in for a meal one Saturday evening with his charming wife, Linda.

A week before the next leg of the competition, each committee had held their respective meetings. The second leg – or summer leg – comprised of the usual requirements for the competing villages to be pristine, clean and attractive, but this time each village had to create an extra-special floral feature on their village greens. They had to be stunning, both in concept and execution.

Maryam and Vincent were jointly in charge of the West Barton village green display, while in East Barton the job had fallen to Ethel and Cecilia.

Maryam and Vincent had designed a beach-themed floral display. The pale-yellow sand would be created by planting out cosmos, the sea would be light blue cornflowers, the dark blue sky made with lobelia and the sun would be formed with gerberas. On the sand, they had designed a flamboyant beach umbrella. It had a real wooden pole laid down among the cosmos and the multicoloured sections of the umbrella itself would be made from red, white, and blue miniature roses.

Ethel and Cecilia, meanwhile, had chosen to represent sailing boats in their floral display. They'd also used lobelia, but theirs was for the dark-blue sea. The sky was light-blue nigella and their sun had been created with dahlias. The hulls and masts of the three sailing boats had been formed with bark chips, and the different coloured sails were made from red geraniums, green chrysanthemums, and orange roses.

They all worked feverishly hard, planning and then planting out their respective designs and displays.

The afternoon before the next day of judging, everyone was putting the final touches to their displays and each team was quietly confident of getting back into the running after the disasters of the first leg. Once the masterpieces were finished, everyone went home secure in the knowledge that they'd done their utmost best. Nothing could possibly go wrong.

8.

Later that night, thick clouds rolled in and brought with them a steady drizzle. By 2am in the morning, the clouds had blocked out all the stars and there was no moonlight at all. It was pitch black.

The eerie quiet was abruptly disturbed by the sound of an engine roaring to life. The engine belonged to a ride-on mower and a dark silhouette was hunched down in the seat, navy-blue gloved hands gripping the steering wheel. The mower was heading straight for East Barton village green. When it was at the edge of the green, a lever was pulled and the cutting deck hummed into action. The mower rode straight across the middle of the sailing boat flower display, scything out a three-foot-wide section of the magnificent creation as it went. It made a quick turn and then came back across with a wiggling motion, so more of the display was torn to pieces.

The driver had to be quick. Lights in nearby houses

were starting to come on as people were woken by the ruckus. The cutting deck was disengaged and the ride-on mower was put into full throttle as it slogged off as fast as it could out of the village. It just managed to be gone by the time anyone reached their front doors.

At the exact same time in West Barton, a faint high-pitch whining could be heard approaching the village. Within only a few seconds, the whining noise was very much louder. A Scrambler motorbike with a rider garbed up entirely in black suddenly raced into the village and roaring past sleepy houses, made straight for the village green at the centre. A Lincoln-green gloved hand firmly squeezed the brake handle and a biker's heavy boot came down, skimming the grass. Aided by the drizzle, the Scrambler executed a twenty-foot-long mud slide right across the damp grass and into the middle of West Barton's fabulous beach-themed flower display. Revving the accelerator madly, the biker then executed a series of devastating doughnut turns that effectively levelled the remaining display and turned the whole thing into a sloppy quagmire.

It was all over in a flash and, as quickly as it had arrived, the Scrambler departed, leaving a trail of devastation in its wake.

9.

'*What the bloody blue blazes!*' came the roar once again, booming loudly across the usually harmonious village of East Barton. The villagers had awoken that morning and, emerging from their peaceful dwellings, were encountered by a scene reminiscent of a war zone. Brigadier Faraday was huffing and puffing up and down the road, shaking his swagger stick furiously towards West Barton and savagely lambasting all the members of their committee.

'Just look at what they've done to our village green!' he raged. 'It looks like they've driven a ruddy tank over it!'

Somehow, the local press had got to hear about the inter-Barton rivalry and were busy taking pictures of the ruined flower display. One of them had made the mistake of asking "Mr Faraday" if he would like to make a comment for the record and was currently being hauled over the coals for addressing him incorrectly and gross insubordination to boot, by Jove!

The competition judge was sensibly keeping his distance from the irate brigadier, especially as he was busy scoring the display a resounding zero out of ten. He just couldn't understand what was going on, but it was more than his job's worth to get involved. He just judged what he saw and what he saw was dreadful.

Ethel was staring at the remains of the display and tutting and harrumphing to herself. The hangdog look on her face said it all. Cecilia was genuinely shocked and upset. All the hard work they'd put into it! Gone in an instant! Bernie and Molly were trying their best to comfort her.

In West Barton, the scene was not dissimilar. The four committee members and half the population of the village were standing next to their village green. They were staring wide-eyed at what looked like a re-enactment of the Somme. The carefully manicured lawn and beautiful flower display were now a mud pit.

Poor Maryam had burst into hysterical tears when she'd seen what had happened to her lovingly crafted display. Richard was clumsily trying to calm her. Vincent's face was set in its usual sneer. Only a slight twitch of his left eye gave away any emotion coursing through his morbid soul.

The competition judge was hiding behind a tree. Having scored the display zero, she was trying to make her way back to her car without running into the fearsome Mrs Barrington-Smythe. She needn't have worried as Cynthia had gone to call Sergeant Richards as soon as she'd clapped eyes on what was clearly another episode of vandalism. She had badgered Fakenham Police Station for a direct number following the previous incident and the sergeant had reluctantly agreed to give her his work mobile number.

The judge just made it back into her car as Cynthia reappeared from making her call. The judge slowly sank down in the driver's seat and disappeared behind the dashboard. Cynthia had clocked her, but was far too preoccupied to be concerned with the blasted woman just now.

Sergeant Richards had been on his way to the police station when he'd received the call from Cynthia. He was passing close by, so he told her he'd come along straightaway. True to his word, he pulled up next to the village green just a few minutes later. His arrival prompted a nervous-looking woman in a nearby car to pop up from behind her steering wheel, start her engine and drive off like the clappers. He wondered what that was all about.

As soon as he set foot out of the squad car, Cynthia pounced. 'So, Sergeant,' she said triumphantly, 'it would appear you were wrong and, despite your warnings, the vandals have struck again!' She pointed a bony finger towards the village green.

Dale turned to look at the devastation. He had to admit, someone had really gone to town this time.

'And it was committed the night before the judging. How do you explain that if it wasn't deliberate and premeditated vandalism?' she asked.

Dale had to concede she had a point. He opened his

mouth to reply, but was saved from having to answer by a static hiss from the radio at his side.

'Sarge?' said a tinny, foppish voice. It was Constable Crowther.

Dale grabbed his radio. 'Richards here,' he replied.

'Just had a call from East Barton, Sarge—'

'Don't tell me!' said Dale wearily. 'Another case of vandalism, right?'

'That's right, Sarge, but how did you know?'

'Call it intuition,' said Dale cryptically.

'You what?'

'Never mind. I'll deal with it. Richards, over and out.'

'Roger.'

He hung the walkie-talkie back on his belt, took a deep breath and turned to address Cynthia and her committee. 'Right,' he said, 'I'm going to sort this out, once and for all.'

'Glad to hear it,' said Cynthia snootily. 'And I presume by that statement that you're going over to East Barton to formally charge them.'

'No, Mrs Barrington-Smythe, I'm not.'

'What the deuce do you mean?' demanded Richard, who'd been dying to stick his oar in.

'If I charge them, then I must charge you, too,' explained Dale.

'But we haven't done anything,' protested Maryam.

'Haven't you?' asked Dale. 'Then who's been doing the vandalism in East Barton?'

They all looked open-mouthed at him. They hadn't thought of that.

'Listen,' Dale continued, 'I've got an idea how to resolve this. Leave it with me and I'll be back in touch soon. I'm going over to see Brigadier Faraday and his committee now, and I'm going to be saying exactly the same thing to them.'

'But, but...' whimpered Vincent.

'Just trust me,' said Dale, with a knowing smile. 'I'm a policeman.'

And with that, he went back to his car and set off for East Barton. He'd just passed The Barton Arms when he noted a car with the logo of the local press going the other way. *Great,* he thought, *that's all we need.* They were bound to have a field day with this story and his name would get dragged into it, no doubt. *Best of luck interviewing Mrs Barrington-Smythe, though,* he mused, with a wry smile.

He pulled up by the village green in East Barton and found Brigadier Faraday liaising with his committee. They were still inspecting the damage and discussing who, in the despicable West Barton committee, was the culprit. Currently, although Cecilia very much rejected the notion, Cynthia's son, Michael, was their main suspect.

'Now you can pack that in!' Dale scolded them as he overheard the conversation. 'You have no proof. Besides which, their village green has been obliterated, too.'

'Really?' asked the brigadier, looking astonished. For once, he was lost for words.

Ethel chirped up instead, 'Well, I can assure you, DCI Richards, that—'

'Sergeant Richards,' corrected Dale. Ethel had obviously been watching too many detective programmes.

'Oh, sorry,' she continued, 'but I can assure you, Sergeant Richards, that no one in this village would stoop so low as to resort to such mindless hooliganism.'

'I wouldn't be so sure,' said Dale. 'How about you?' he said, turning towards Bernie.

'Me?' said Bernie, looking horrified.

Dale consulted his notepad. 'It says here you're a Mr Rolls. A farmer.'

'That's roight,' said Bernie.

'Well, then, you'd have all the necessary equipment to plough up a village green, wouldn't you? It'd take seconds.'

'I would never use Royce for ought like that!' protested Bernie.

'Royce?' enquired Dale.

'She's moi little tractor. So as oi can tell folk I drive a Rolls-Royce, y'see. Just a bit of fun.'

'I see,' said Dale, 'but nonetheless you had the equipment and motive to carry out the crime.'

'I never did nuthin' o' the kind!' remonstrated Bernie. 'You tell 'im, *Brigadoon*!' He looked pleadingly at the brigadier to back him up.

The brigadier decided to overlook the misuse of his rank for the time being and rounded on Sergeant Richards. 'Just what the devil do you think you're playing at?' he clamoured. 'You can't go around accusing innocent men of wrongdoing like that!'

'My point exactly. Because that's precisely what you've just done to Mrs Barrington-Smythe's son,' said Dale. He patted Bernie on the shoulder. 'Don't worry, Mr Rolls, I don't really think you committed any crime. I was just making a point.'

Bernie looked mightily relieved.

'So,' continued the sergeant, 'you can see how these things can get out of hand. Now, with your blessing, I think I have a solution to this little problem. It'll take a little organising, but, if you bear with me, I'll be in touch as soon as I can.'

They murmured their agreement and Dale returned to his car and got in. He turned the Mondeo round and drove back the way he'd come. He had one more visit to make and one hell of a favour to ask.

Half a mile down the road, he stopped the squad car in the car park of The Barton Arms. He got out and went up to the entrance door of the pub. Being only 10:30am, it was still too early in the day for the pub to be open, but he could hear a vacuum cleaner whining away inside, so he knocked loudly on the door and waited for a response.

The vacuum cleaner was switched off and presently Jenny unlocked the front door and peered outside. On seeing Dale and the squad car, she looked a little concerned.

'Hello, Dale. Is everything alright?' she asked.

'Not exactly,' said Dale. 'They've been at it again, I'm afraid. The villages.'

'What do you mean?'

'East and West Barton. They've trashed each other's village greens. All over this Best Kept Village Competition or whatever it is.'

'You're kidding me!'

'I wish I was,' he said, sighing. 'Listen, I'm sorry to disturb you, but can I come in for five minutes for a little chat?'

'Of course you can,' said Jenny. 'Come on in and I'll get the kettle on. I'll get Keith for you. He's just cleaning the beer lines. You go and get a seat in The Snug and we'll be along as soon as.'

As Dale stepped into the pub, Jenny called out to her husband, 'Keith! Dale's here to see us. You'll never guess what's happened!'

Keith's head popped up from behind the bar. 'How do, Dale,' he greeted him, 'what's been going on then?'

Keith went over to sit with Dale in The Snug and Jenny soon joined them, bringing three mugs of tea with her. Dale filled them in on all the sordid details of what had happened.

'Well, they're clearly all off their chumps!' said Keith once he'd heard the story.

'You're telling me!' said Dale. 'But somehow, I've got to try and sort this out. I've got an idea, but I need your help.'

'Go on,' said Jenny.

'Well, I was thinking about arranging a meeting between the two committees, face to face, to try and get them to talk rationally to each other and sort all this out,' explained Dale. 'It'd have to be somewhere neutral, though.'

'Like where?' asked Keith.

'Like here. At your pub,' said Dale. 'It's the perfect place.'

'It is, is it?' said Keith. He didn't look overly enthralled.

'*And* I'd need you to be the mediator,' added Dale with a slight wince.

'Bloody hell, Dale. Can't you do that? You're the policeman after all.'

Dale held his hands up. 'The best I can do is set it all up, but I can't be directly involved when they all meet up. I don't think my superiors would approve, if you know what I mean.'

'I suppose not,' Keith acknowledged.

'Will you help me then?' Dale implored.

'Yes, of course we'll help you,' said Jenny.

Keith nodded, but he had a grim look on his face.

10.

Keith and Jenny had agreed to host the meeting between the two villages on the following Wednesday evening at 8pm. Sergeant Richards had written official letters to both committees, inviting them to attend the evening with a view to solving the current situation. Any concerned inhabitants of either village interested in attending would also be most welcome. He had received prompt replies from both committees advising that they were willing to do so and would post a copy of the letter on their respective village noticeboards to inform people of the meeting.

The sergeant was very pleased that his plan was going well and that people were being cooperative. He dropped by The Barton Arms on the Wednesday afternoon to give Keith and Jenny a few pointers and to wish them luck. Following Sergeant Richards' advice, Keith had set up tables on each side of the bar room. The west side of the bar room for the West Barton committee and the east side for the East Barton committee. *Seems logical*, he thought. Jenny was going to work the bar and Keith was going to act as mediator. Everything was ready.

As 8pm approached, one of Vincent's luxurious black limos pulled up outside the pub. It looked very presidential and Cynthia was especially pleased when Vincent got out and opened the door for her, Maryam and Michael. Richard, following close behind, had elected to arrive in his top-class 4x4 as usual. He parked alongside them and they entered the pub together.

Shortly after, Bernie, Molly and Bill arrived in the huge pickup truck, while Ethel and Cecilia had accepted a lift in the brigadier's vintage Jag. They, too, entered the bar and, ignoring the already seated West Barton committee, made their way to their own seats on the east side. Quite a few villagers had made their way up to the pub earlier and were already seated and politely waiting for the proceedings to start. Keith and Jenny were ensuring that everyone had ordered drinks and been served before formally starting the meeting.

When he was sure everyone was settled, Keith went behind the bar and came back holding a folded newspaper. Dale had provided it for him earlier. He walked to the gap in the centre of the bar room between the two committees and cleared his throat to get everyone's attention.

'Welcome, ladies and gentlemen,' he began, 'and thank you for attending the meeting this evening.' He paused momentarily. 'And in case anyone is unaware,' he continued, '*this* is the reason we are all here!'

He unfolded the newspaper, revealing it to be the *Fakenham Guardian*, and brandished the front cover at both committees in turn. The headline across the front page ran:

THE WAR OF THE ROSES!

Underneath, there were pictures of each of the village greens, showing the floral displays before and after the chaotic incidents in question. There were also some random mugshots of committee members, looking surly and bad-tempered. There was an audible shocked gasp from both sides of the room.

Keith lowered the newspaper, folded it back up and put it down on the bar. 'So,' he said, 'Sergeant Richards has instructed me to act as a mediator tonight and to try and resolve the issue. He has suggested that we start with each committee – or individual, as the case may be – confessing to the acts of vandalism that we've all been witness to. The meeting is entirely confidential and the sergeant has assured me that no charges will be pressed.'

He gave a serious look to each side. 'Who'd like to start the ball rolling?' Leaving it at that, he sat himself down on one of the barstools and waited.

There was an awfully long silence, with the odd cough and shuffling of feet. No one seemed to want to break the ice.

The brigadier, unsurprisingly, was the first to lose patience. 'Come on!' he glowered at the West Barton committee. 'Just own up. We all know it was one of you lot that wrecked my clematis. I have my suspicions.'

'And just what do you mean by that?' retorted Cynthia, whose patience had also been running thin. 'And what about my tulips? Which one of your lot did it? You?'

She pointed vaguely at the East Barton committee, but Bernie, perhaps being overly sensitive after his run-in with Sergeant Richards, thought she was implicating him.

'Oi never touched yer rotten ole flowers. I'm jus' an honest farmer. A Norfolk man, born and bred, strong in the arm—'

'And thick in the head!' She finished the rhyme for him. 'We all know *that* bit!'

'Don't you speak to moi 'usband like that!' warned Molly. 'Us Rolls can't be pushed too far!'

'Well, you said it,' smirked Vincent. 'Too many sausage rolls by the look of him. It's no wonder you need that Yank tank to go around in.'

That pushed it over the edge. Ethel lost her rag. She didn't like to see her friends insulted. 'Och, look everyone,' she said, joining the fray and pointing at Vincent, 'we've found the *Berk*. But where's *Hare*?'

'Are you suggesting I'm some sort of body-snatcher?' queried Vincent snidely.

'Well, you certainly look unnatural. *Nosferatu* springs to mind,' said Ethel, looking pleased with her putdown.

Richard, eager to vent off some of his own pent-up

vitriol, decided it was time to join in. 'That's a bit rich, coming from *Jimmy Krankie*'s granny,' he guffawed.

'How dare you!' said Ethel, looking affronted.

'Look,' said the brigadier, 'can we just get on—'

'Oh, yes,' cut in Richard, 'let's hear from *Sergeant Bilko* again.'

The brigadier started to turn red with irritation. 'Now, you listen to me, bloody *Lord Snooty*. I wouldn't be surprised if it wasn't you behind the destruction of our village green,' he fumed accusingly.

'I'll have you know I'm a well-respected pillar of the community,' refuted Richard, drawing himself to his full height.

'Pillock of the community, more like,' chortled Bernie, pleased he'd got one in on the arrogant pratt. He'd never liked Lord Braithwaite.

The villagers who'd come up to attend the meeting couldn't believe their luck. This was first-class entertainment. They were looking eagerly from side to side, waiting for the next sucker punch to land. They didn't have long to wait.

Keith tried to restore order. It wasn't going at all well. 'Now, can we all just calm down?' he said. 'This isn't helping.'

'Well, *I'm* perfectly calm,' said Maryam, who was indeed completely composed and serene. 'And I just want to point out the extensive damage done to the habitat of the flora and fauna living on the village greens. There may have been birds nesting and hedgehogs—'

'Oh, give it a rest, *Doctor Dolittle!*' Ethel berated her. 'This isn't an episode of *Wildlife Rescue*.'

Maryam sat back in her chair, looking disappointed and distraught.

'Will you get that Highland Terrier under control!' Cynthia seethed at the East Barton committee.

Ethel glared at her, but was met with an equally chilly stare.

'Now!' said Cynthia, changing tack. She fixed the brigadier with a look of cold contempt. 'I believe we were about to hear a confession?'

The brigadier wasn't about to fall for that old trick. 'Nice try, *Maleficent*,' he said sweetly, 'but you'll be hearing no such thing from me.'

The next hour of the evening progressed in a similar fashion, with each side trying to force a confession from the other, but it was all to no avail. Keith was getting exasperated with the lack of progress.

Cecilia had felt sorry for poor Maryam when she'd been shot down in flames for bringing up the issue of wildlife. She thought she ought to follow her lead and try a more measured approach. 'Listen, everyone,' she began, 'we have to learn to get on together.'

'Well said!' came a voice across the room. It was Michael. Cynthia shot him a warning glance.

'If we're going to live in harmony,' Cecilia continued, 'we have to be singing off the same hymn sheet. We all need to be playing the same tune!'

'Well, you're an accountant, so we all know you'll be

good on the fiddle!' jeered Vincent, unable to control himself.

Cecilia rolled her eyes and pouted in annoyance. There was an appreciative chuckle from the audience of villagers who were having a whale of a time. Bernie wasn't so amused.

'What did you say to her, *Igor*?' he asked threateningly.

'*Igor*?' questioned Vincent. 'Surely you can do better than that, being a man of such high education?'

'Oi got moi degree from the University of Life!' said Bernie.

'Ah,' said Vincent, 'but did you pass?'

Bernie snapped. 'Roight, *Baron Samedi*, oi've just about heard enough out of you!'

And they were off again. The two committees traded accusations and insults for a further twenty minutes before Keith finally threw in the towel.

'Ladies and gentlemen,' he shouted above the hullaballoo, 'I think our business has concluded for the night. I want to thank you for your attendance.' He gave a nod to Jenny, who rang the bell for last orders. It had the effect of ending the fight and the two committees returned to their corners.

Soon after, people started to disperse. Cynthia stood up to leave and looked around for Michael, who had disappeared. She spied him chatting with Cecilia in The Snug.

'Michael!' she shrilled. 'Leave that girl alone and get over here. We're leaving.'

He reluctantly got to his feet and, waving goodbye to Cecilia, he made his way over to the door and trailed out of the pub after his mother.

'Cecilia!' growled the brigadier, not to be outdone. 'Must you talk to that upstart?'

'Oh, Uncle, do stop. He's a lovely man,' she said, taking the brigadier by the arm. They made their own way out to the car park where the rest of the committee were waiting. After a few minutes, all the cars were gone and the pub was empty once again.

Jenny and Keith were cleaning the last of the glasses behind the bar.

'Well, that was an unmitigated disaster,' said Jenny.

'Yep', said Keith.

They switched off the lights, locked up and turned in for the night.

*

The next morning, Dale telephoned the pub from his office at the police station.

Keith answered the phone. 'The Barton Arms.'

'Morning, Keith,' said Dale, 'I'm just ringing to see how last night went.' He was optimistic that a solution had been found.

'Morning, Dale,' replied Keith. 'I'm sorry to disappoint you, but it didn't go very well at all.'

'Oh, no! Well, what happened? Did no one admit to anything?'

'Not only did no one admit to anything, but the

whole thing just turned into a three-round slanging match.'

'Oh God,' lamented Dale, 'not a clean fight then?'

'Put it this way: in round one, the gloves were off and they were punching below the belt from the start!'

'No way!'

'It was quite an insight actually – they really hate each other, I can tell you.'

'And round two?'

'It was a no-score draw. Plenty of points scored, but no one came out as a clear winner.'

Dale was pleased Keith didn't seem angry about the failure and was being jovial about it. He continued the light-hearted banter. 'And round three? Any KOs?' Dale laughed.

'It came close! At one point, I thought the big farmer bloke was going to deck that ugly skinny guy.'

'That'd be Bernie Rolls and Vincent Kleeb. Who'd have thought they'd be bar-room brawling! You couldn't make it up!'

'I know,' chuckled Keith, 'life is stranger than fiction sometimes!'

'Ah, well, I really appreciate you trying. Seems this is going to be a tougher nut to crack than I thought,' said Dale.

'Yeah, it could be, I'm afraid. It could be.'

Dale thanked Keith and Jenny again, and then hung up.

Jesus wept, he thought, *what am I going to do with that lot?* Well, he wasn't going to do anything much more at the moment. He had far more pressing police matters to deal with. He put the file on the back-burner for now.

11.

As the summer rolled on, the rivalry and hatred between the two villages carried on growing. No one from either village would speak to each other. The only ones who wanted to liaise with one another were Cecilia and Michael, and they'd both been heartily discouraged from doing so – not that they let that stop them. They carried on their secret meetings in the churchyards all summer long. They'd fallen in love.

The decimated village greens had slowly been repaired over several months. More modest flower displays had been replanted, and the turfed areas had been rolled and reseeded. They looked as good as ever.

In mid-September, both the WBBKVC and the EBBKVC held their respective meetings for the next phase of the competition. The third – or autumn – part of the competition centred around a special feature being presented by each village. In East Barton, this was Bernie's pristine bowling green and in West Barton, it was Richard's magnificent, personalised hedge. Given the atrocities that had been committed during the previous two legs of the competition, both committees had raised concerns about ensuring the safety of their special features. They'd both written to the long-suffering Sergeant Richards with their concerns and a list of their demands.

*

The following evening, Dale was up at The Barton Arms enjoying a quiet drink and having a good chinwag with Keith about it. There was no one else in the pub.

'So, they wrote letters to you, did they?' asked Keith with a grin on his face.

'They did indeed,' said Dale, 'and you wouldn't believe what they were demanding.'

'Try me.'

'Well, that Cynthia Barrington-Smythe and Richard Braithwaite were demanding the police cordon off the entrance to his lordship's estate – with barbed wire, no less!' said Dale with a wry smile.

'I'm surprised they didn't ask for an electric fence! With watchtowers!'

'I know!' replied Dale, laughing. 'And it gets better.'

'Go on, what did the other side want?'

'Oh, that was far simpler. Brigadier Faraday and Mr Rolls only wanted half a dozen police officers to stand guard over the village bowling green all night – that was all.'

'Armed police, no doubt!'

'I didn't dare ask! Besides, the brigadier's probably got a machine gun nest set up by now!'

'So, what did you tell them in reply?' asked Keith, still chuckling at the idea.

'I told them the police do not have the resources for that kind of activity. I told them that if they want me to get involved again, I'd need evidence. Not just random accusations. Real evidence.'

'How are they going to do that?' enquired Keith.

'Well,' explained Dale, 'I told them to spy on each other the night before the judging day. You know, stake out each other's houses and make sure no one's up to no good. And if they find anyone up to no good, then to perform a citizen's arrest and take lots of pictures. And then to inform me and I'd take it from there. You never know, they might even crack the case for me!'

'Yeah, right!' Keith laughed. 'In your dreams!'

'I know!' said Dale with a smile.

He stayed chatting with Keith for another ten minutes and then left to go home. The pub was empty once again.

12.

A few days before the third leg of the competition, Cynthia arranged for an extraordinary meeting of the WBBKVC to take place. She'd received the reply from Sergeant Richards and while she had been disappointed that the police were unwilling to help as much as she'd like, she was pleased with the further suggestions he'd made. She had interpreted the policeman's instructions to mean that her committee was effectively being deputised to help catch the criminals responsible. And she intended to do just that. There was no doubt in her mind who was to blame. Clearly, it was the EBBKVC.

The meeting was being held at Barton Hall. They'd agreed it was the safest place to meet, away from prying eyes. Cynthia had left Michael at home. Given his relationship with Cecelia, he couldn't be trusted not to blab. Maryam and Vincent sat opposite Cynthia and Richard at one end of a vast oak table in the hall's immense ornate dining room. Richard had given the staff the night off, to be extra sure the meeting was secure.

In a rare act of humbleness, he personally served each of his guests with a brandy, while he was nursing his customary malt whisky. The chandelier was dimmed to a low light and a fire was crackling in the fireplace. It was a bit like a meeting of *SPECTRE*.

'As you all know,' began Cynthia, 'Sergeant Richards has instructed us to help catch the culprits of these obscene acts of vandalism.'

'Damn right!' chipped in Richard.

'Thank you, Richard,' she said curtly. 'Now I have a plan to catch them at it. We will follow Sergeant Richards' suggestion to spy on them the night before the judging. It's bound to be when they plan to attack. However, we are obviously all well known to them, so if they see any of us, it'll blow the whistle. We need to be disguised.'

'Excellent,' said Vincent, 'but won't this be in the middle of the night? That's when the other attacks took place.'

'Quite right, Vincent. So, what I'm proposing is that we disguise ourselves as tourists; if anyone asks, we can say we're lost and looking for our holiday accommodation.'

'What kind of tourists?' asked Maryam, who wasn't looking at all sure about this plan.

'Oh, I don't know,' said Cynthia, shrugging. 'French?'

'French!' blurted Richard. 'I'm a Lord of the Realm! I can't go around dressed up like some garlic-infused pompadour!'

'Well, what do you suggest, then?' she asked sourly.

'Well… I, I, I…' he stammered.

'Right, you'll be French then!'

'Oh, very well,' he moaned. 'I'll be a bloody frog, if you insist.'

Cynthia moved on. 'I propose we communicate on the night by mobile phone. I know we all have one and I know everyone's number. Let's take the precaution of setting the phones on silent mode. I suggest we do it now to be sure.'

They all produced their mobiles and made the necessary adjustments.

'The other problem we have is transport. We can't use one of Vincent's cars for obvious reasons and everyone would recognise Richard's. And I don't drive…'

Maryam looked wary. She knew what was coming. All heads turned her way.

'What do you drive, Maryam?' queried Cynthia innocently.

'A Peugeot,' she whimpered.

Cynthia's eyes lit up. 'A French car! Oh, perfect, that's settled then.'

'What is?' asked Maryam.

'I could make some fake French licence plates to put on,' suggested Vincent.

'Good idea,' agreed Richard.

'Now, just hold on a moment,' protested Maryam. 'I've got a very responsible job in this community. I'm a doctor, for goodness' sake. I can't drive round with illegal plates!'

'This *is* for the good of the community, Maryam,' lectured Cynthia. 'I'm sure the authorities will just see it as a necessary means to an end in the capture of these awful criminals.'

'Well, if you're sure,' said Maryam, caving in.

'Of course, I'm sure,' Cynthia reassured her. 'So, we're all agreed on the plan. I suggest Maryam picks us up at 1am at the village hall. That should give us time to get over to East Barton and get in position. Everyone got it?'

'Got it,' they all said in unison.

'Good! And don't forget to be disguised!'

The meeting broke up and they made their way home. The trap was set.

*

On receiving the reply from Sergeant Richards regarding the security of the next phase of the competition, the brigadier had immediately called for a *COBRA* meeting with his own committee. The sergeant had made it clear that due to lack of police resources, he would be struggling to catch the saboteurs unaided. He was obviously reaching out to the brigadier's military expertise in order to expedite the capture of the offenders in question. Brigadier Faraday had naturally risen to the challenge.

He had been about to call Cecilia when he'd thought better of it. She was in collusion with that Smythe boy and would probably give the game away. Instead, he called Bernie and asked if Molly would be prepared to step in. Bernie had said it'd be no problem. And so, the meeting had been arranged for a week's time at 9pm in the village hall. It gave the brigadier time to formulate his strategy.

A week later, the revised committee members were all in attendance and the brigadier had locked the village hall door and pulled down the blinds. He wasn't about to let any Herberts barge in and snoop on his plans.

The brigadier had set up a whiteboard behind his desk and had drawn a rough map of West Barton on it with a felt-tip pen. He'd marked the locations of the various suspects' homes upon it. Utilising his swagger stick as an impromptu pointer, he commenced his briefing.

'Right, troops,' he affirmed, 'as you can see, this is a map of the enemy camp.'

'It looks like West Barton to me,' said Ethel.

'Precisely!' asserted the brigadier. 'That's where the saboteurs are lurking – and we've got to fish them out.'

'Ow are we gonna do that, then?' asked Bernie.

'We will place our operatives in the marked locations for surveillance purposes,' he explained, pointing at the whiteboard with his swagger stick. 'And as soon as the swines make their move, we'll nab them! We know the previous acts of sabotage were carried out at approximately 2am, so, ideally, we need to meet here at 1am and get ready. We can then head over to West Barton to carry out the operation. Any questions?'

'Who are our operatives?' asked Ethel.

'Er, well, now, of course I knew you'd all volunteer

without hesitation and I wouldn't dare insult you by making a formal request,' said the brigadier. He looked to the horizon with misty eyes and his voice was tinged with fervour. 'You've made an old soldier very proud! Well done!'

'You mean it's us, then?' asked Ethel with a sigh.

'Well… yes,' he admitted. 'And actually, we'll be needing your car, too.'

'Och, jings!'

'Won't we be recognised if we're spotted?' asked Molly.

'Good question!' answered the brigadier, relieved that someone had changed the subject. 'And you can leave that to me. You don't spend forty years in the army without learning something about camouflage – what! I will supply this on the night.'

'How are we going to keep in contact with each other when we're at different posts?' queried Bernie.

'Simple!' replied the brigadier. He rooted around in the knapsack he had under the table and pulled out four handheld VHF radios. 'Thought these would come in handy one day. I've preset them all to channel 10. All you have to do is switch them on. But remember to keep the volume low!' He handed out the radios and they all had a quick practice. Everyone seemed to have great confidence in the brigadier's plan. He beamed happily at them. This was just like the good old days!

'Right,' he said conspiratorially. 'Meeting adjourned. I'll see you all in a few days here at 1am. And wear something practical, 10–4?'

He gave them the thumbs up and they gave the thumbs up back. He unlocked the village hall door and let them out.

13.

It was the early evening of the day before the third leg
– or autumn leg – of the competition. Richard had just
finished overseeing the final trimming of his hedge and
Cynthia had gone over to inspect it. She had to admit
his groundsmen had done an exemplary job. It was
stunning. The rest of the committee had been fussing
round the village, making sure everything else was
perfect for the next round of judging.

As night drew in, they all returned home as normal
so as not to arouse any suspicions. They all had their
evening meal and then turned in early, just as they
had in the last two rounds. This time, however, it was
a pretence.

Later that night, there was a little flurry of activity.
It was five minutes to 1am and Cynthia was waiting
by the doors of West Barton's village hall. Her disguise
consisted of a simple dress, belted round her waist, a blue
beret pulled low over her right eye and a chiffon scarf

that she could use to part-cover her face, if necessary. Simple, but perfect.

Vincent was the next to turn up. His rather forthright approach to a disguise was to be the absolute stereotype of a Frenchman. He wore a blue-and-white striped jersey, black trousers and a red spotted neckerchief. To hide his thinning greasy black hair, he'd also opted to wear what appeared to be a 1960s mop-top wig. He looked like an estranged French relation of the *Addams Family*. Cynthia was relieved, at least, to see he was not carrying a full string of onions round his shoulders, nor did he have a baguette tucked under his arm. *Some small mercy there*, she thought.

'Good evening, Vincent,' she hailed him. 'You look… interesting.'

'Bonsoir,' he replied with a crooked grin.

Maryam arrived next, at the wheel of her Peugeot. She had on a headscarf and her face was heavily made up with blue eyeshadow, rouged lips and powdered cheeks. It seemed to Cynthia that she'd gone for the Gallic gypsy look. It was very effective.

Vincent produced two identical white rectangular pieces of paper. Both had numbers on and white and blue "F" emblems located at each side. He'd printed them off earlier. These were the fake French licence plates he'd promised and he attached them with sticky tape over the car's existing plates. *Et voilà!* Job done.

Last to arrive was Richard. He came meandering up the street towards them wearing a full-length light-beige raincoat with the collars turned up round his face.

Under his nose, he'd attached a huge drooping black moustache. Cynthia wasn't at all sure what look he was trying to achieve, but he looked suspiciously deviant.

'Evening all,' he said amiably.

'You look like a pervert,' she greeted him.

'Well,' he replied, somewhat bemused, 'they have perverts in France, don't they?'

'I think they invented it,' said Vincent, who'd read some *Marquis de Sade* once and been utterly appalled.

'Right then,' said Cynthia, looking at her watch, 'I think we'd better get going. Did everyone remember their phones?'

'Yes,' they all chorused.

'Good, let's go then,' she ordered. 'Richard, I think it best if you sit in the back with me; Vincent, you go in the front passenger seat. And remember – try to look *normal*!'

They all piled in and Maryam pulled the Peugeot gently away from the curb, then headed east down the Old Barton Road.

*

'Blast it,' muttered Brigadier Faraday as he struggled to turn on his pen-sized LED torch. He finally managed it and then, having located his keys, he let himself into East Barton's village hall. It was a quarter to one in the morning. He wanted to pull down the blinds before switching on the hall lights, so no one would see the hall was in use. Once he'd accomplished the task, he closed the front door and then switched on just enough lights to be able to see by. He was wearing his full battledress kit from his army days. He had on camouflaged trousers, a khaki shirt and a green jumper with reinforced elbow and shoulder patches. His black boots had been brushed and polished, and were positively gleaming.

He set out the equipment he'd brought with him on the desk. As well as his torch, there were the four VHF handheld radios, a digital camera and some sticks of green, brown and black camouflage face paint.

There was a faint knocking on the door. The brigadier went over and opened the door a crack to peep through. It was Bernie and Molly. They'd been working most of the afternoon rolling, mowing and strimming the village bowling green ready for judging day. It was now looking absolutely perfect. As he let them in, he was pleased to see they'd dressed sensibly in light-green farm overalls.

'Well done, you chaps!' he whispered. 'Take a pew while we wait.'

Bernie and Molly sat down and eyed the equipment on the desk with interest. The brigadier held a finger to his lips to indicate for them to stay quiet. They nodded their understanding. Presently, there was another knock on the door.

'Cooee!' called Ethel loudly. 'I'm here!'

The brigadier shot up and rushed over to the door to let her in. 'Shh!' he hushed her. 'Are you trying to wake the whole village?'

'Ooh, sorry,' she said in a muted tone.

As she walked in, the brigadier, Bernie and Molly caught sight of the outfit she was dressed up in and stared at her in shocked surprise. She was wearing a two-piece plaid suit consisting of a tweed jacket, matching plus fours, knee-length socks and sensible leather walking shoes.

'Ethel,' said Molly in a low voice, 'what on earth is that get-up you've got on?'

'You look loike you're about to tee off at the Old Course of St Andrews!' added Bernie.

'What do you mean?' queried Ethel, looking abashed. 'Brigadier Faraday said to wear something practical – plus fours. So, that's what I've done.'

'Hell's bells!' hissed the brigadier. 'I said to wear something practical. 10–4!'

'Och, crivens! Well, you know I don't hear so good these days.'

'Look, never mind,' said the brigadier. 'At least you're in green. Let's get on, shall we?' He walked back to the desk and picked up the camouflage sticks.

'What's that for?' asked Ethel suspiciously.

'Well, if we don't want to be recognised,' he replied, waving the sticks at them, 'then this is our best bet. Who's first?'

Bernie felt somehow honour-bound to be the first to volunteer, so he stepped forwards and said, 'Go on then – do yer worst.'

The brigadier began to apply the paint to Bernie's face. He started with the brown, which he was applying to look like an earthy base. 'Now, the trick with camouflage is to apply it randomly,' he explained. 'You don't want to be putting it on in fancy striped patterns like you see in these Hollywood films.' He moved on to the green paint stick and added some patches of undergrowth to complete the base. Then, to finish, he added a few thinner strokes of the black paint to look like twigs. The brigadier took a step back to admire his handiwork. He was very pleased. 'Next!' he commanded.

Rather reluctantly, the two ladies went through the same procedure, with the end result being equally as successful as Bernie's transformation.

Molly volunteered to apply the camouflage to the brigadier. She copied how he had done it very carefully and, when she'd finished, she was pretty chuffed with the result.

'Ahem,' smirked Bernie, who was trying not to laugh. 'Oi think yer may 'ave missed a bit.' He was diplomatically trying to point out the now rather luminous bald dome of the brigadier's head. It stuck out like the top of a hard-boiled egg.

'Oh, yes. Silly me,' said Molly and quickly slapped some more paint on, so as not to cause the brigadier any further embarrassment.

'Thank you, me dear,' he said appreciatively. 'And now I think we'd better make tracks. Is the car ready?'

'It's parked outside my house, just over the road,' said Ethel.

'Right! Let's go then.'

The brigadier handed out the VHF radios and put the other items in his knapsack. They quietly exited the village hall, carefully turning off the lights behind them. Standing in the darkness and with the camouflage on, they were almost invisible. They crept over the road and made their way to Ethel's house.

Her car was a jovial yellow colour and was of a design that the manufacturers like to refer to as 'compact'. In other words, it was tiny. She only ever used it to go to the local shops. It had four seats, but it was a two-door model, so you had to press a lever and slide the front seats forwards to get in the back.

The brigadier was surveying the car with a dubious eye. After considering the logistics of the matter, he decided that unbridled optimism was probably the best way forward. 'Molly and Bernie,' he whispered, 'if you can slink into the back seats, then I can sit in the front to direct things—'

'Slink!' muttered Bernie. 'Oi'll give meself a bloomin' hernia tryin' to get in there.'

'Nevertheless, if you could please attempt it. Time is pressing on – what,' urged the brigadier.

Approaching the car from either side, Bernie and Molly gave it a shot. They successfully managed to get a leg each in the back seat, but attempting to squeeze their overly ample posteriors between the front car seat and the side of the car door was proving to be vexing.

'Are you managing it?' asked the brigadier impatiently.

'No, oi've only got one cheek in,' replied Bernie.

The brigadier, aware of the delay this was causing, was starting to lose his cool. 'Allow me to aid you,' he insisted. 'On three. Ready?'

Bernie looked concerned, but nodded.

'One… two…' He grabbed hold of Bernie's shoulders and gave him an almighty shove. 'Three!'

Bernie shot backwards, accompanied by a terrible ripping sound, and landed in an ungainly fashion on the back seat.

'Oi jus' split moi trousers in two!' he complained from the depths of the car.

'Well, you've got your overalls on,' stated the brigadier. 'No one will notice.' He turned his attention to Molly.

'Oh no you don't!' she warned. 'Oi'll sort meself out.'

With a combination of Ethel pushing and Bernie pulling, Molly was eventually manoeuvred into the back seat with slightly more aplomb.

The front seats were then pushed back, adding further to Bernie and Molly's discomfort, and presently the brigadier and Ethel took their places in the front seats. The combined weight of the committee members was pushing the little car's suspension to the limit. It was almost touching the ground.

Ethel started the car, put it in first gear and let the clutch out. Gingerly, the little car moved off and made its way towards West Barton. Every time there was a bump in the road, there was an awful scraping noise as the car's undercarriage came into contact with the road and a shower of sparks flew out behind it.

For once, the brigadier was grateful for Ethel's hearing problem, as she was blissfully unaware of the atrocious damage being sustained to the underside of her cherished little car.

They slowly made their way out of the village and headed west along the Old Barton Road. About halfway to the pub, the brigadier was surprised to see the headlights of another car heading towards them. As they passed by, he just managed to glimpse the registration of the car and noted it was French. *They must be totally lost to be driving around at this time of night*, he mused. *Poor blighters.*

*

In Maryam's Peugeot, they were just approaching East Barton when the lights of a car materialised in front of them. It seemed to be a very small car and they didn't recognise it, but it was clearly having mechanical trouble. It was moving very slowly and every now and again, it appeared to be catching on fire. Being a kind-hearted lady, Maryam would normally have stopped and offered assistance, but tonight, of course, that would be impossible. They passed by and headed into the village.

The first stop was Ethel McKinley's terraced cottage. Vincent was duly ousted from the car and posted to watch her house for anything suspicious. Cynthia let herself out near the brigadier's house, while Richard was deposited next to the village phone booth, which was located opposite Cecilia's home. The phone booth was of the traditional red design and provided the only source of light in the otherwise dark village. Now everyone was in position, Maryam drove just a little way out of the far side of the village where the entrance gates to the Rolls' farm were located. She turned off the car headlights, switched off the engine and watched for any sign of activity.

*

In West Barton, the brigadier had just been dropped by the entrance of Barton Hall while Ethel, Bernie and Molly had gone back into the village and parked up next to the churchyard. From here, both Dr Jahan's and Vincent Kleeb's residences could be seen. To save Bernie and Molly the palaver of getting out of the car again, they had opted to stay put and do their spying in situ. Ethel had got out and was walking the short distance to Mrs Barrington-Smythe's cottage. She was doing her best to make use of any natural foliage and ducked down next to a nearby hawthorn hedge. With the help of the camouflage, she was very hard to spot indeed.

Everyone held their positions, monitoring the various properties. Fifteen minutes passed with no activity.

'Gold Eagle, Gold Eagle calling all troopers. Come in. Over!' fizzed the brigadier's voice over the VHF radio. There was quite a pause before anyone replied.

'Go ahead, Bald Eagle,' said Bernie, giving a wink to Molly. She tried not to crack up laughing.

'That's *Gold* Eagle,' came the tetchy reply.

'Who's Gold Eagle anyway?' asked Ethel.

'It's me. Faraday. Who'd you think?' responded the brigadier irritably.

'Well, you ne'er told us you were Gold Eagle,' said Bernie.

'Can I be the Tartan Flyer then?' added Ethel.

'Oh, well, if we're all 'avin nicknames, we wanna be Momma Bear and Poppa Bear,' chipped in Molly.

'Has everyone quite finished?!' huffed the brigadier. 'Never mind about names! Can everyone just report in? I'll start. There's no sign of life from Barton Hall. No lights on. Nothing at all.'

'Nuthin 'ere either,' said Bernie, 'but there's no car on the doctor's drive, mind.'

'Hmm, that's strange.'

'Someone's in at Cynthia's,' whispered Ethel. 'There's a light just come on.' She observed the sleepy figure of a man walk by one of the windows. 'I think it's Michael. Just got up to use the bathroom at a guess.'

'Doesn't prove anything,' stated the brigadier. 'She's the one we're after and we haven't seen her or any of the others.'

'So now what?' Ethel put the question to him.

The brigadier gave the problem some thought. He had the feeling there was something not quite right here.

'Where would the good doctor be driving to in the middle of the night?' he mused. 'Unless…'

'Unless we've missed them somehow,' Bernie finished the thought for him.

'And they're all over in East Barton – doin' goodness knows what!' said Molly excitedly.

'Blast!' erupted the brigadier. 'Quickly! Back to the

car and come and pick me up. We've got to get back as soon as possible!'

Ethel popped up from the hedgerow and trotted back to the car as fast as she could. Climbing in, she started the car and drove as rapidly as the overladen car would allow to rendezvous with the brigadier. They spotted him marching briskly back towards the village and pulled over to pick him up. The little car turned round one last time, passed through West Barton and then started the drive back east.

'Kill the headlights,' ordered the brigadier.

'What for?' asked Ethel.

'Because we don't want them to see us coming. We're going to catch them red-handed!'

Ethel did as she was instructed and turned off the lights. The brigadier reached into his knapsack and took out his digital camera. He was going to provide Sergeant Richards with all the proof he needed.

*

Cynthia had been staking out the brigadier's house for close to twenty minutes and all was quiet. Very quiet. She decided it was time to find out how the others were getting on. She took out her mobile phone and made a group call to all the committee members. Within a few seconds, they had all joined the group conversation.

'Has anyone seen anything suspicious?' she enquired of them.

'Nothing going on here,' replied Maryam.

'Not a sausage,' said Vincent.

'Sod all here either,' added Richard grumpily, 'and I'm getting damned hot in this raincoat.'

Cynthia thought it a little odd that there was absolutely no sign of life whatsoever from any of the properties. She wasn't sure what to do, but they needed to know one way or the other what the situation was. She quickly formulated a desperate and daring plan.

'I'm going to ring Brigadier Faraday's doorbell,' she informed them.

'You what?' exhorted Vincent. 'What if he catches you?'

'I'll just have to make sure he doesn't, won't I?' she replied testily. 'I'm going over. Stand by your phones.'

'Good luck!' said Richard.

Feeling like a naughty schoolgirl, she covered her face with her scarf, sneaked up to the brigadier's front door and pressed the bell. There ensued a huge cacophony of various bells and chimes, which seemed to last forever. Cynthia turned on her heels and, mustering as much composure as she was able, made off hastily down the path, then hid behind the stone wall. There was no way anyone could sleep through that racket, she reasoned. She waited a full minute, but no lights came on and no one came to the door.

'He's not in!' she told them. 'And that can only mean one thing...'

'Oh God!' wailed Richard. 'They'll be after my hedge!'

'Maryam! Quick! Get back here and pick us up!' instructed Cynthia.

'I'm on my way!' said Maryam.

She started the car and headed back into East Barton as fast as she dared. She went to pick up Cynthia and Vincent first, with Richard to follow.

As he waited to be picked up, Richard was starting to fret about his beloved hedge. He was sweating profusely and getting visibly anxious and twitchy. He was getting so hot he unbuttoned his raincoat and began flapping it open and closed in an attempt to cool himself down. He saw with relief that the car was approaching.

*

Moments earlier, Cecilia had awoken, convinced she could hear voices outside. Curious, she got out of bed and padded over to the window. She pulled the curtain aside slightly and took a peek across the road. To her horror, she could see a dreadful miscreant wearing a grubby raincoat standing next to the phone box. He was clearly lit and she distinctly saw him pulling his raincoat open and flashing at a passing car of French tourists. She quickly closed the curtain again. *The poor things*, she thought. *What a terrible thing to happen on your holiday*. She made up her mind to call Sergeant Richards first thing in the morning to report the foul degenerate to the police.

*

Maryam pulled over and Richard clambered into the back passenger seat.

'Step on it,' he panted. 'My hedge is in great peril!'

Maryam duly obliged and set off at speed back to West Barton.

'I think we should turn the headlights off,' suggested Cynthia, 'because if they see us coming, they'll run for it before we can catch them.'

'Good idea,' agreed Richard.

Great, thought Maryam, *now I can be arrested for illegal plates and dangerous driving.* But she turned them off anyway.

*

Ethel's little yellow car was about to reach The Barton Arms, when, out of nowhere, the French registered car they'd encountered earlier came flying out of the darkness at terrific speed, heading straight for them. Ethel managed to swerve off to the left in the nick of time and went sliding across the gravel at the entrance to the pub. They came to a halt in a cloud of dust.

The French car also veered off the road and slewed onto the grass verge, where it eventually came to a stop about fifty yards further up the road. The shocked occupants of both cars began to slowly emerge from their vehicles.

Suddenly, the security lights of the pub flared into life, partially lighting up the sorry scene. Keith and Jenny, woken by the commotion, had come out of the front door of the pub wearing their dressing gowns and slippers. Keith had a flashlight in one hand, which he pointed towards the little yellow car. The light flickered across the figures of four heavily camouflaged individuals who were standing in a huddle nearby.

'Who are you then?' enquired Keith. '*The Dirty Dozen*?'

'I'll thank you not to take that tone with me!' said the brigadier, flaring up. He'd recovered from the shock of the near miss and was trying to gather his wits.

Keith thought he recognised the voice. 'Is that you, Gerald?' he asked in surprise. He flashed the light over the other three figures. 'And Bernie and Molly. And *Ethel*? What in the name of God are you all doing dressed up like *Rambo*?'

'We were on our way to stop another round of sabotage – that's what we were doing, by Jove! And we'd probably have caught them at it, too, if we hadn't been run off the road by those dashed Frenchies driving around in the middle of the night with no lights on!'

Keith turned his attention to the French car and shone his light towards the odd-looking group standing on the verge.

'And what do we have here?' queried Keith, looking a bit bemused. 'The cast of *'Allo 'Allo*, by the looks of it.'

'Let me speak to them,' said Jenny. She had spent a year in Paris on a foreign work exchange program. Her French was almost fluent.

'*Ça va*?' she shouted over to them. '*Quelqu'un est-il blessé*?'

'Er, *bonsoir*,' came the reply from the small man wearing an unconvincing wig.

'*Votre voiture est-elle barrée*?' she tried again. '*Avez-vous besoin d'aide*?'

'*Bonsoir*,' was the strangled reply again.

'What's going on then?' Keith asked.

'Well,' explained Jenny, 'it would appear we have a French car full of French people who can't speak French!'

'Why are you driving at night with no lights?' Keith questioned them.

'*Bonsoir*.'

'Oh, knock it off, Vincent. You're not fooling anyone,' snapped the lady wearing a beret.

'Vincent? Vincent *Kleeb*? Is that you?' asked Keith. He suddenly realised who the lady was. 'And Cynthia? And presumably Richard and Maryam, too?'

'Thank God I can finally take this bloody coat off,' griped Richard, undoing the buttons of the raincoat and removing his false moustache.

'But why are you all dressed up like the French Resistance?' questioned Jenny.

'We're in disguise,' explained Cynthia, 'as we have been attempting to catch that lot in the act of vandalism. And by the looks of them, they have clearly been up to no good!'

'That's a bit rich looking at the state of you!' growled the brigadier. 'And where exactly have you been? Ruining our bowling green, I'll wager!'

'We have done no such thing!' retorted Cynthia with indignation.

'And I'll bet you lot were vandalising my hedge!'

accused Richard angrily. A thought flashed into his mind and, grabbing his mobile phone from his pocket, he quickly set it to camera and took a picture of the brigadier and his colleagues.

'There!' proclaimed Richard triumphantly. 'Now I have evidence!'

This only prompted the brigadier to produce his own digital camera and take a picture in retaliation.

'And so do I!'

This, in turn, induced both sides to produce cameras and phones and start taking pictures at random in a wild flurry of flashes.

Keith was rapidly losing patience and could see that things were progressing nowhere fast. 'Could we all just settle down?' he hollered at them. 'And stop taking bloody pointless pictures!' Thankfully, he managed to get through to them and, after a few more errant flashes, they soon desisted.

'I strongly suggest you all get back in your cars and go home!' he continued. 'By all means, check there's been no foul play to any property, but then *please* get yourselves to bed!'

Moaning and groaning, the two committees reluctantly returned to their vehicles. Maryam's car left first. After a few minutes of pushing and shoving, Bernie and Molly were reinstated in the back seat of Ethel's car and they, too, set off. Ethel's car no longer scraped the ground, but it was now making a very throaty clamour instead. This was due to the fact that her exhaust pipe had not survived the near collision and had parted company with the car altogether. It was lying on the pub's driveway, but in the near darkness no one had noticed.

Maryam dropped Richard by the entrance gates of Barton Hall. He wanted to be absolutely certain his hedge was intact. They could all see that it was fine. He waved goodnight to them, shrugged and walked off up his driveway to the hall.

Well, thought Cynthia, *we may not have caught the vandals red-handed, but we have certainly thwarted their plans.* Maryam dropped the rest of the committee off and drove home. She was exhausted.

*

In East Barton, Ethel parked up outside her home and the committee walked the short distance up to the church and onto the adjacent bowling green. The brigadier shone his torch all around the area. There was nothing to see. The bowling green was as perfect as when it had been left several hours ago. At that, they called it a night, happy in the knowledge they'd succeeded in foiling any attempt of sabotage. The brigadier and Ethel returned to their respective homes, while Bernie and Molly walked the short distance out of the village and up the drive to their farmhouse.

14.

About an hour later, a car silently pulled up close by the entrance gates to Barton Hall. A figure clad all in black emerged and went to the boot of the car. Opening it, a hefty chainsaw was lifted out, along with a ten-foot length of thick rubber hose, a bucket of water and some Lincoln-green gardening gloves. The equipment was taken over to the nearby majestic hedge. Having put on the gloves, the rubber hose was then attached to the exhaust of the chainsaw and the other end of the hose went into the bucket of water. Then, the chainsaw was started. You could only faintly hear it. The rubber hose assembly was essentially acting as an improvised muffler. It worked well. The figure set to work cutting through various trunks of the hedge that formed the letters of Richard's name. As each individual trunk was cut, they were given a firm push and they fell back onto the park-like lawns of the Barton Hall estate. Within a quarter of an hour, the job was done, the equipment packed away and the car was gone.

Almost simultaneously, an intruder dressed all in black was walking along the bowling green in East Barton. At the back of the green was situated an old disused field gate, which in turn gave access to a cattle-run. The cattle-run wound its way to another gate, which opened onto the flowing fields where the Rolls dairy herd were peacefully grazing. The bolt of the field gate was slid back by a hand wearing a navy-blue glove and, with some difficulty, the gate was pushed back until wide open. The figure then walked up the cattle-run and opened the second gate onto the fields. Making some strange clicking noises, the attention of some of the nearby dairy herd was attracted. Being curious animals, the cows eagerly followed the mysterious interloper back down the cattle-run and out onto the bowling green. Satisfied that at least a dozen cows had come through onto the green, the field gate was pulled closed and bolted once again. The figure then exited through the main entrance gate back onto the road and melted into the darkness.

15.

It was half past seven in the morning and Sergeant Richards was still asleep when his mobile phone started ringing. He knew today was the third instalment of the Best Kept Village Competition and he'd been expecting and dreading a phone call. Linda tutted and rolled the covers over her head as Dale sat up and answered the phone. The call was from Cecilia Dawson, but to his surprise it was not about the competition. She was ringing to report that a depraved pervert had been at large in East Barton last night, apparently flashing at passing cars. He took down a description of the offender and promised her he'd look into the matter as soon as he could.

Over breakfast, he fielded another call. This time, it was from The Barton Arms. Keith had rung to fill him in on all the details of the crazy escapades that had occurred outside the pub last night. Dale had nearly choked on his coffee. But he was intrigued that Keith's account of Lord Braithwaite's 'disguise' was a suspiciously close match to the description of the phone-box flasher provided by Ms Dawson. He ran Cecilia's story through with Keith and it was Keith's turn to choke on his coffee. But he agreed with Dale that there was an incredible similarity in the two descriptions. When he finally hung up, Dale shook his head in disbelief.

'What's happened?' asked Linda, looking concerned.

'You wouldn't believe me if I told you,' he replied.

'It's those nutters from East and West Barton again, isn't it?' she hazarded a guess.

'Yep,' sighed Dale. He rose from the kitchen table, gave her a kiss on the cheek, went down the hall and opened the front door.

'Have a good day!' she called after him with a laugh.

'I'll see you later,' he smiled and closed the door.

He drove the Mondeo into Fakenham and parked up in front of the police station. On entering the main reception hall, PC Josh Crowther was grinning at him from behind the front desk. Dale was not in the best of moods to be dealing with Josh this morning.

'What are you smirking at?' he glowered.

'Just taken some calls for you, Sarge. You'll never guess where from…'

'Christ on a bike! I've already had two calls for incidents at the Bartons this morning!'

'Well, now you've got two more!' snickered Josh.

'Right,' said Dale testily, 'well, you can wipe that cheesy smile off your face, my lad, 'cause guess what?'

'What?'

'You're coming with me!'

'What? Why me?' wailed Josh.

'Call it work experience. I'll give you five minutes to get ready and then join me out in the car park. Got it?'

'Yes, Sarge,' replied Josh mardily.

'And you can stop looking at me with a face like a slapped arse an' all!'

Josh huffed off to the locker room to get his gear. He met Sergeant Richards five minutes later by the squad car. Dale was waiting for him behind the wheel. Josh got in the passenger side and gave Dale a weak smile.

'Don't worry, lad,' said Dale. 'Just follow my lead, keep your trap shut and you'll be fine.'

He turned on the flashing lights and they set off for the Bartons. He thought it best to deal with Ms Dawson's complaint first, it being the most serious, so they made tracks for East Barton.

Ten minutes later, they pulled up outside Cecilia's terraced cottage. She was waiting at the door for them. As they walked up the entrance path, she opened the door wider and they went in and were shown through to her sitting room.

'Would you like a tea or coffee?' she enquired sweetly.

'Ooh, lovely—' began Josh.

'No, thank you,' cut in Dale, giving Josh a stern look. 'We won't take up much of your time. In fact, I've a feeling we can clear this matter up fairly quickly.'

'Oh right,' said Cecilia, looking pensive. 'That's good, I suppose.'

Dale produced his notepad and flicked through

a few pages. 'You provided me with a very accurate description of the offender, Ms Dawson, thank you. But I was wondering if you could also provide me with a description of the victims?'

Cecilia thought for a moment before replying. 'Well, it was all very quick. It was definitely a French car. I remember seeing the licence plate.'

'And the occupants?'

'Well, there was a frightfully ugly little man in the front seat wearing a striped jersey, I think. And a lady who looked a bit like a gypsy. She had a headscarf on. I couldn't clearly see the person in the back.'

'And who was driving the car?'

'The gypsy lady, I'm sure.'

'Okay, good,' said Dale. 'One more question, though.'

'Go ahead,' said Cecilia, wondering where the sergeant was going with this line of questioning.

'Now, think carefully. When you were looking at the car as it approached, which side of the car was the lady sat on?'

'Well, she was nearest to the awful flasher, so she was on the left side,' said Cecilia.

'Can you think of anything odd about that?' asked Dale.

'I don't follow you.'

'Well, you said it was a French-plated car.'

'Yes.'

'But if she was on the left side as the car came towards you, then the vehicle would be a right-hand drive. In other words, a British car.'

Cecilia worked it out in her mind and realised that the sergeant was correct. 'Oh, yes,' admitted Cecilia. 'That is odd, isn't it?'

'Well, it would be,' sighed Dale, 'apart from that I happen to know a Peugeot belonging to a Dr Maryam Jahan was being driven in the vicinity late last night with false licence plates.'

'What? Dr Jahan? Whatever for?'

'It's a good question,' said Dale. 'I'm led to believe that Dr Jahan and her colleagues had disguised themselves as French tourists in an attempt to catch the criminals who have been vandalising the village displays over the last year.'

'Dr Jahan was disguised as a French gypsy? Are you joking?'

'Sadly. No.'

'So, the ugly little man was—'

'Vincent Kleeb,' Dale finished the sentence for her.

'And the person in the back seat?'

'Cynthia Barrington-Smythe.'

Cecilia was beginning to put two and two together. 'So, the awful man in the raincoat was—'

'Lord Richard Braithwaite.'

'Not a flasher?'

'Not that we know of.'

'Well, what was he doing flapping his coat open and closed?'

'I can't be sure of that – maybe to attract their attention?'

'Oh, I feel a bit silly now,' murmured Cecilia.

'No need to feel silly, Ms Dawson. It was entirely correct of you to report the incident.'

'But how do you know how all this happened?'

'Well, this is where you're esteemed uncle enters the plot, I'm afraid.'

'Sorry?'

'Well, it would appear that there was a near collision that occurred to the vehicle of Dr Jahan late last night, just outside The Barton Arms.'

'And what has this to do with my uncle?'

'Your uncle was a passenger in the other vehicle involved in the near miss. Along with Bernie and Molly Rolls and Ethel McKinley.'

'The committee? Goodness, are they all alright?'

'Physically, they're fine,' Dale reassured her. 'Mentally, well, that's another question.'

'What do you mean?' she asked, slightly affronted.

Dale sighed again and took to flipping through his notepad once more. 'Well, according to the witness statement provided by Mr Atkins, they were all wearing camouflage and dressed up like commandos.'

'They were?' she asked in disbelief.

Dale nodded. 'I'm afraid so. They also claimed they were doing so in order to catch the aforementioned vandals.'

'I see… I think,' said Cecilia, who was utterly confused.

Dale rose to his feet and Josh followed suit. 'Well, thank you, Ms Dawson. I hope you appreciate I needed you to identify the car belonging to Dr Jahan. It was necessary in order for me to clear up the facts of what occurred last night. I hope this has been brought to a satisfactory conclusion regarding your complaint.'

'It has. Thank you, Sergeant.'

'And now, I fear we must attend to another incident we have received a call-out for regarding the village.'

'Oh, yes, I did see a lot of people were gathered up by the churchyard,' said Cecilia.

'Indeed,' stated Dale, 'we'll be walking up there now.'

'May I come with you?' enquired Cecilia. 'I feel I ought to find out what's going on.'

'Of course you can.'

Dale nodded to Josh and they led the way out of the house, closely followed by Cecilia. Together, they walked the short distance up to the church. There were about twenty people gathered around the churchyard and the adjacent bowling green.

As they reached the churchyard, Dale was sure he could hear the lowing of cattle. As they passed through the gate, they were astounded to discover at least a dozen cows standing grazing on the bowling green. They had made a complete and utter mess of it. The bowling green was a mass of cow hoof divots, mud and torn-up turf. There was also a good smattering of cowpats.

Molly Rolls was leaning against the stone wall. Her eyes were red as she'd obviously been crying. She looked terribly upset. Cecilia rushed over to her and put her arm around her to calm and comfort her.

Dale turned to Josh and whispered to him to go and

help her. Josh nodded and made his way over to assist. Dale, meanwhile, went looking for Bernie Rolls. He passed Ethel McKinley on his way, who scrutinised him unfavourably with a pug-faced grimace. Dale ignored her.

He found Bernie standing with his head resting on the forehead of one of the larger cows. The cow was regarding him balefully.

'Oh, Gertrude, what 'av yer done?' Bernie lamented.

Gertrude mooed softly in reply.

'Mr Rolls?' Dale said gently, to get his attention.

Bernie shifted his head so that he could look at Dale.

'May I have a word?' Dale asked.

Bernie stood up straight and gave his full attention to Dale. 'Of course, Sergeant. Thank ye for comin' over so quick.'

'That's okay. No problem. So… can you tell me how you think this happened?' enquired Dale, taking out his notebook once again.

'Well, it were no accident, Sergeant,' said Bernie. 'I can tell you that for nuffin. The gate at the back there was bolted closed and the one on moi fields, too. They've both been opened during the night. The cows will have jus' come straight down the cattle-run. Simple, really.'

'You think it was done with the intention to cause deliberate damage?'

'No doubt about it. These here cows weigh more than half a ton each. If enough were let through, they was always gonna trample the place. They can't help it. Just big lugs.'

'I see,' said Dale. 'I'm truly sorry, Mr Rolls.'

'The bit tha' gets me, though, Sergeant, is that they used me own bloody cows to do it! Tha's a bitter pill to swallow, that is.'

Dale patted the big man on the back and left him to his sorrow. He made his way back to the entrance gate and beckoned Josh to join him.

'Not much else we can do here,' he said. 'Time to move on.'

'Right, Sarge.'

As they exited the bowling green, they almost bumped into Brigadier Faraday, who had just arrived on the scene to take stock of the latest fiasco. The brigadier looked annoyed and Dale was expecting an unpleasant confrontation. To his surprise, though, the brigadier was uncharacteristically charming.

'Dashed bad show – what!' he remarked, taking in the disorderly scene.

'It certainly is,' agreed Dale.

'Any luck finding the culprits?' asked the brigadier innocently.

'Not yet,' admitted Dale.

'They are certainly slippery customers, I'll grant you. We came very close to catching the blighters ourselves last night, as a matter of fact.'

Dale could see where the brigadier was headed. 'Really?' said Dale, matter-of-factly. 'As I understand it, you came very close to killing yourselves in a head-on collision.'

The brigadier puffed out his cheeks and went a

darker shade of red. 'You heard about that, did you?' he asked guiltily.

'I did, yes,' replied Dale.

'Well, look here, damn it, at least we were trying! I mean, isn't it obvious to you who's responsible for all this?'

'Go on, enlighten me.'

'Surely it has to be the West Barton committee! Who else?'

'It's a theory, I'll give you that,' stated Dale, 'but as I've told you before, until I have concrete evidence, I will not be making any arrests.'

The brigadier harrumphed and glowered angrily at the sergeant for a moment. He then turned on his heels and spying the hapless Best Kept Village judge, made a beeline for him instead. The judge saw him coming and desperately looked around for a means of escape, but he was too slow. The brigadier bore down on him.

'What score have you awarded us?' he demanded of him.

The judge had been a bit flummoxed, as he'd been expecting to appraise a pristine bowling green, but instead had only encountered a small dung-filled paddock full of cows. Hardly a horticultural highlight. 'Erm, well, zero actually,' he whimpered.

'What the bloody blue blazes are you thinking, man?' bawled the brigadier, as he began haranguing and berating the poor fellow mercilessly.

Sergeant Richards and PC Crowther chose that moment to make their exit and hastily strode back to the squad car. Josh had been impressed how the sergeant had handled things so far this morning. Once they were safely back in the car, he told Dale as much.

'Thank you, lad,' said Dale appreciatively. 'You're not doing so bad yourself. But we're not out of the woods yet.'

They drove off towards West Barton, passing The Barton Arms on the way. They slowed down a little by the pub to survey the evidence left from the near collision the night before. They could clearly see where the cars had gone off the road. A discarded exhaust pipe was still lying on the pub's gravel drive.

They carried on, passing straight through West Barton, and pulled up close to the entrance gates of Barton Hall. As they took in the view through the squad car windscreen, both Dale and Josh could not help bursting out laughing.

The splendid topiary display adorning the entrance to Barton Hall had been somewhat altered. The magnificent hedge had once read:

RICHARD BRAITHWAITE ESTATES

But thanks to the removal of some of the letters, the hedge now read:

RICH   T WA T ESTATES

The policemen practically fell out of the car in hysterics. Tears were rolling down Josh's face and Dale was doubled up, holding his stomach.

'Are you quite finished?' asked the disgruntled voice of Lord Braithwaite as he stepped out suddenly from behind one of the entrance gate pillars.

Dale looked up in surprise and tried his best to compose himself. 'Our apologies, sir,' he said with a shaky voice, 'we were just sharing a private joke in the car.' Indicating the hedge with an outstretched arm, he continued, 'This, of course, is a most serious matter.'

Josh snorted uncontrollably and set Dale off in fits again.

Lord Braithwaite waited impatiently for them to regain their composure. He glared at them with a seething sneer of displeasure. Josh and Dale eventually pulled themselves together, and then stood in awkward silence while Richard continued to glare. Finally, he deigned to speak.

'I fully intend to press charges,' he informed them. 'I know exactly who has done this. I know their motive. And, what's more, I have evidence.' He had the attention of the policemen now, he noted.

'You have evidence, sir?' asked Dale eagerly.

'Yes, I do,' smirked Richard. 'I thought that would wipe the smile off your faces.'

Dale produced his notepad and hastily found a pen. 'If you would care to give me a formal statement, sir,' he said seriously.

Richard was beginning to enjoy his moment in the limelight and began to strut about like *Hercule Poirot*. 'As I suspected all along,' he began smugly, 'the culprits of this crime are the East Barton Best Kept Village committee members. More precisely, Gerald Faraday, Ethel McKinley, Bernard Rolls and Molly Rolls. Further collaborators may also include Cecilia Dawson and Bill Rolls, but, unfortunately, the evidence I have at this time does not indict them.'

'I see, sir,' said Dale, who was going along with the charade for the time being. 'And the motive?'

'Simple. By destroying my hedge – and by extension, West Barton's horticultural highlight – they were removing any serious challenger in the Best Kept Village Competition, thereby teeing themselves up for a unanimous victory.'

'Very good, sir,' chimed Dale. 'And now if I may enquire exactly what evidence it is that you have to substantiate these theories.'

'Not theories, Sergeant. Facts!' preached Richard.

'Your evidence, if you please,' persisted Dale.

'I have photographic evidence showing all four of them using camouflage and wearing clothing complicit in carrying out this crime. *And* they were caught heading on their way directly to the crime scene.'

'May I see the photo, please?' asked Dale.

'Certainly!' said Richard primly and reached into his pocket to find his mobile phone. He went into the camera setting and flicked through various photos in the album, before deciding on one and handing it over to Dale.

Dale took a look at the photo. The four camouflaged members of the East Barton committee were, indeed, captured on the photo, lit up by the flash like startled rabbits. In the background, you could see the pub and their small yellow car on the drive. The time and date of the picture was also digitally imprinted on it.

'There you are, you see,' smarmed Richard. 'Caught bang to rights.'

'There may be a few issues with this, sir,' suggested Dale.

'Oh? Such as?'

'Well, their yellow car for one, sir.'

'What of it?'

'You claimed you caught them heading to West Barton to commit the crime.'

'Yes.'

'It is clear from the position of the car, with reference to The Barton Arms in the background, that this car is heading towards *East* Barton.'

'But—'

'Also,' continued the sergeant, 'the time that the photo was taken is digitally imprinted here at 01:53. According to the statement of Mr Atkins, it was surmised that no damage had been suffered to any property in either village prior to this time.'

'Ah, well, you see—' spluttered Richard.

'So, in fact,' explained the sergeant, handing him his camera back, 'your photo actually proves their alibi at that time and exonerates them from any blame.'

Richard gave the sergeant another vitriolic glare.

'Anything else you'd like to add?' asked Dale, calmly.

'Yes,' replied Lord Braithwaite, moodily. '*Bugger!*'

The sergeant rolled his eyes, flipped his notepad

closed and returned it to his pocket. To add insult to injury, the Best Kept Village judge sent to assess West Barton's horticultural highlight chose that moment to drive by. She didn't even bother stopping the car. She took one look at the hedge, pulled a face in disgust and simply held up a piece of card to the window with the number zero marked on it.

'*Bugger*!' scowled Richard again. 'Cynthia's going to have someone's head on a platter for this. Probably mine...'

Dale was studying the hedge and looking pensive. 'Listen,' he said, 'I may have an idea how to catch the offender.'

'You do?' said Richard, brightening a little. 'Well, crack on, by all means.'

'It's a bit of a long shot, but bear with me, okay?'

'Okay,' said Richard, but he didn't look overly hopeful. He turned his back on them and began the walk back up his drive to Barton Hall.

'What's the plan, then?' enquired Josh.

'You'll find out soon enough,' replied Dale. 'Let's get back to the station.'

They jumped back in the Mondeo and drove back to Fakenham. When they were back in the police station car park, Dale beckoned Josh to follow him. They went round the side of the station to the rear of the police compound. Right at the back was where the K9 unit was based.

'You around, Mick?' called Dale to the collection of decrepit outbuildings.

A scuffling noise came from one of the sheds and then the shabby form of PC Mick Granger appeared from the gloom, holding a battered tin mug of tea in one hand. He held the other hand over his eyes to shield them from the sudden sunlight. Mick was a local man. For years, he'd shepherded sheep on various farms in Norfolk, before joining the police force to specialise in dog handling.

'That you, Sarge?' he asked. 'What can I do you for?'

'There's been a serious incident of vandalism up at Barton Hall,' explained Dale. 'It must have taken whoever did it quite some time, so I'm hoping one of your dogs would get a good scent and be able to track them down.'

Mick scratched his stubbly chin and gave it some thought. 'You'll be wanting Jack, then, I reckon,' he decided.

'Jack?'

'The bloodhound. He's been trained to pick up a scent, track it down and then hold the offender in custody until the police arrive.'

'Hold the offender in custody?' questioned Josh. 'How does he do that?'

'You'll see. Don't you worry, he's fully trained,' said Mick.

'Can you have him ready in about half an hour?' asked Dale.

'Sure I can,' said Mick. 'I'll get him togged up in his K9 police dog gear and have him ready in the van. Meet you in the front car park at 1pm. How's that?'

'Perfect,' said Dale.

While Mick got Jack ready for duty, Dale and Josh went down to the canteen and grabbed a quick bite to eat.

'This morning was a lot more fun than being on the front desk,' enthused Josh between mouthfuls of his sandwich.

Dale had to admit it hadn't been dull. 'It's not always like this, lad,' he warned. 'Sometimes I have to deal with sane people.'

Josh chuckled.

At 1pm, they met PC Granger in the car park as arranged. Jack was in the back of the dog unit van, looking sorrowful and dribbling down the rear window. They set off in convoy back to Barton Hall. The Mondeo led the way with the dog unit van following behind. They pulled up by the entrance gates where Dale and Josh had been an hour or so before. There was no one about, so Mick put a lead on Jack and led him straight over to the spot where the hedges had been vandalised.

'Someone's got a sense of humour, ain't they?' laughed Mick as he read the altered letters of the hedge.

Josh and Dale grinned and nodded back at him. Mick let Jack get a good sniff of all the cut hedges and of the ground that surrounded the immediate area.

'I think he's onto something,' exclaimed Mick, excitedly. 'Good boy, Jack!'

The bloodhound's nose was almost on the ground and his tail was wagging madly. Mick was struggling to hold him.

'Let him go for it,' said Dale. 'We're ready to follow.'

'Right you are, guvnor,' said Mick with a smile and unfastened Jack's lead.

They were expecting the bloodhound to lead them along the road and into the villages, but instead the dog shot off up the drive of Barton Hall and then veered off and disappeared into the extensive grounds.

*

Lord Braithwaite was sitting in his favourite wingback armchair, sipping his third double malt whisky of the day from a finely cut crystal tumbler. Even he didn't usually start drinking this early of an afternoon, but he'd had a very stressful morning. He was staring out of the huge leaded glass window of his sumptuous drawing room. From here, he could see all the gardens and parkland to the front of the hall, right down to the entrance gates.

As he sat surveying his estate, out of the corner of his eye he thought he could see movement down at the far end of the grounds. And then he was certain he saw a large dog bounding across the end of his drive. *So,* he brooded, *some fearful oiks think they can just walk over my property, letting their bloody dog roam all over the place. Well, they've got another thing coming.* He was going to teach them a lesson they'd never forget.

'Jenkins!' he yelled at the top of his voice. 'Fetch me my shotgun.'

Jenkins was Barton Hall's long-serving butler. He'd been with the Braithwaite family for decades.

'Yes, milord,' he chanted and scuttled off obediently to do Richard's bidding.

Richard heaved himself out of the chair and walked over to the patio door. He opened it and went out onto the huge terrace. The terrace was stone flagged and decorated with various antique statues of a biblical nature. The statues were his grandmother's doing. She'd been devoutly religious. There were also several ornate stone urns planted with a rich variety of flowers and grasses. He took up position behind a particularly large urn, which was sprouting some voluminous pampas grass. It provided him with some natural cover as he tried to locate the mangy mongrel that was trespassing over his property. Jenkins promptly joined him and presented him with the shotgun. Richard checked it was loaded, cocked it and slipped on the safety catch.

He scoured the grounds and soon spotted the dog's tail waving about in one of his prized decorative flower beds. He raised the shotgun to his shoulder and levelled the dog in his sights. Once he had a bead on him, he lowered the shotgun slightly so that he was aiming at the grass about ten feet away from the beast. He was going to give him the fright of his life.

'Have at you, you brute!' he whispered as he released the safety catch.

There was a gap between the flower beds and, as the dog passed from one to the other, Jenkins caught a fleeting glimpse of the black-and-white chequered police logo on the dog's protective coat.

Just as Lord Braithwaite was about to fire, Jenkins suddenly lurched forward and screamed down his ear: '*Don't shoot!*'

As he did so, he accidentally stood on Richard's foot and sent him reeling off balance. As Richard staggered, the shotgun went off with a terrific bang. The recoil sent him flying backwards, landing him on his back, spreadeagled on the stone patio.

A nearby priceless statue of a cherub playing a harp got both barrels and exploded in a cloud of dust and debris. Only its tiny feet remained; the rest had gone to join the choir invisible.

*

Dale, Josh and Mick were halfway up the drive, desperately looking to see where Jack had got to, when they heard the shotgun go off.

'*Jack!*' howled Mick at the top of his voice. He was extremely concerned the shot had been intended for the bloodhound. The three policemen raced up the drive towards the hall, where the blast had come from.

As it happened, Jack was just fine. Hearing the shot himself, his training had kicked in and he'd made straight for the source of the gunfire as quickly as his gnarly legs could manage. Jack was not bred particularly for speed, but he was surprisingly agile for such a lolloping lump.

*

Lord Braithwaite was slowly regaining his wits. He had just sat upright and was looking around, slightly dazed, when Jack landed squarely on his chest in a frenzied flurry of fur, fangs and slobber. He knocked Richard flat on his back again and before he knew what had hit him, Jack had grasped his trouser leg between his powerful jaws and would not let go. Every time Richard tried to stand, Jack pulled on his trouser leg and prevented him from getting up.

'Help!' squealed Richard. 'Get the wretched creature off me! Jenkins! Help me!'

As Jenkins attempted to approach, Jack gave him a low warning growl. Jenkins was having none of it and backed off at speed.

'Jenkins! I'll have your job for this, you damn coward!' squawked Richard.

The policemen finally arrived on the scene, gasping for breath after sprinting up the last few hundred yards of Richard's sweeping drive. Mick hastily attached a lead to Jack and gave him a powerful tug backwards. The bottom half of Richard's trouser leg, still firmly in the powerful grasp of Jack's jaws, tore off with a loud rip.

Mick manhandled Jack a safe distance away from Lord Braithwaite and got him to sit. Jack spat out the chewed-up remains of Richard's trouser leg.

'Good boy!' praised Mick, giving Jack a treat and scratching his ears.

'Good boy?!' hollered Lord Braithwaite, still flat out on the patio. 'He nearly had my bloody leg off!'

'What a load of ole squit!' Mick rebuked. 'He

wouldn't hurt you. He's a fully trained police tracker dog. Jack the Sniffer, we call him.'

'Jack the Ripper would be more apt,' shouted Richard caustically. 'Just look what he's done to my trousers.'

'The police will pay for the repair,' said Dale sternly. 'What I want to know is what the hell do you think you were playing at?'

'What do you mean?' replied Richard defensively, finally getting to his feet. 'I didn't know you were going to let a dog loose on my property. What were *you* playing at?'

'We returned with the police sniffer dog to try and catch the offender who vandalised your hedge. We were expecting Jack to lead us into West or East Barton,' admitted Dale. 'However, he must have picked up your scent instead. Have you been down by the hedge?'

'Of course I have!' snarled Richard. 'I've been down to inspect the damage.'

'That must be how he picked up the wrong scent,' confirmed Mick.

'I still want to know what you were doing letting off that shotgun. Were you trying to shoot Jack?' Dale asked suspiciously.

'Lord Braithwaite was merely trying to scare the hound away, sir,' interjected Jenkins, who was desperately trying to regain favour with his employer. 'He would never deliberately harm a defenceless dog.'

'Thank you, Jenkins, I do like an honest chap to speak his mind. Well said!' beamed Richard.

'Milord.'

'Besides which,' added Richard, 'when I see a dog trespassing off lead, I can only assume he's intent on savaging our rare breed birds.'

'But we don't keep rare breeds, sir,' said Jenkins, unwittingly putting his foot in it.

'Shut up, Jenkins!' barked Richard. 'When I want your opinion, I'll dashed well ask for it. Got it?'

'Milord.'

There was a brief period of silence while everyone got up to speed with the goings-on. Eventually, it was Josh who broke the peace.

'Now what?' he asked.

'I think we'd better call it a day,' said the sergeant. He turned to talk to Richard directly. 'I'm sorry it didn't work out with the sniffer dog. It was worth a try, though. Do send us the bill for your trouser repair. And please mind what you're doing with that shotgun of yours in future!'

'Very well,' said Richard. 'Will do.'

'We'll be returning to the station now. I'll be filing my report in due course. And, of course, we will continue with our enquiries,' Dale informed him.

'Very good, Sergeant,' murmured Lord Braithwaite. He handed the shotgun back to Jenkins. 'Put that away, will you? And when you've finished tidying up that statue, I'll be in need of another drink.' He sauntered off into the house, leaving the butler looking peeved.

Dale gave Jenkins a sympathetic nod and then they look their leave. The three policemen and the police dog began the walk back down the drive to their vehicles.

Jesus, Mary and Joseph, thought Dale. *What a hell of a day.*

Josh, on the other hand, had thought it'd all been highly entertaining.

16.

Several days later, Cynthia was sat at her kitchen table, drinking a strong black coffee. She needed it. In her hand was a copy of the latest *Fakenham Guardian*, hot off the press that morning, and it did not make for good reading. The main headline had read:

NEW NAME FOR LOCAL SHOOTING GROUND

And a picture of Richard's vandalised hedge was printed underneath. The paper had then gone on to expound on the ongoing feud between the Bartons. A picture of the East Barton bowling green being trampled by a herd of cows had been printed under that.

Somehow, they'd even managed to cotton on to the incident outside The Barton Arms. According to the press, a rampaging horde of French tourists were causing chaos across the district, while a crack platoon of commandos had been spotted carrying out mysterious military manoeuvres in the dead of night. There was also a warning for the public to be on the lookout for a crazed pervert stalking the area, dubbed as 'The Phantom Phone Box Flasher'.

The newspaper had claimed the police were clueless as to what was going on and that they'd declined to comment. They'd printed a picture of Sergeant Richards unsuccessfully attempting to block his photograph being taken with an outstretched hand.

'What an absolute load of tosh!' seethed Cynthia, throwing the newspaper down onto her kitchen table. She had to admit, though, that it was a complete and utter PR disaster for the WBBKVC. God only knows how they were going to pull this back from the brink. It was now all down to the success of the final stage of the competition. Cynthia contacted her committee members and between them they agreed on a date in the last week of November, giving plenty of time for them to plan their village Christmas Party Extravaganza. In the meantime, they'd just have to try and make reparations as best they could.

*

Bernie had managed to drive Royce, his mini tractor, down through the cattle-run and onto the bowling green. He'd attached a lawn roller to the back and had levelled the bowling green as best he could. The lawned surface of the green was another matter. It was too late in the season to re-sow it, so he'd just have to leave it as it was until next spring. Fortunately, the bowling club had finished all their fixtures for the season a few weeks beforehand. Bernie would do his best to get it re-established by early next summer. Realistically, that was the best he could hope for.

*

Lord Braithwaite's vandalised hedge had unwittingly become quite famous. Or, more accurately, infamous. Tourists and locals had been stopping by his gates and taking pictures of themselves by the hedge. Richard soon became fed up with them and summoned his groundsmen to do something about it. They erected a green fabric screen along the front of the hedge. It would stay in place until the hedge was replanted and regrown back to its former glory. That would take years, though, and it irritated the bejesus out of Richard every time he passed by.

*

Business at The Barton Arms continued to be slow. As the bitterness grew more intense between East and West Barton, the business suffered, too. Keith and Jenny made some financial forecasts and concluded that if they continued at the current level of trade, they would go bust before the next summer. Their situation was getting critical.

Like Cynthia, the brigadier had been knocked sideways by the negative stories issuing from the press and local tittle-tattle. He was doing his best to run a damage limitation exercise, but he was probably flogging a dead horse. The damage done to the EBBKVC was severe. He'd called round the troops and asked them to put their thinking caps on to try and come up with something spectacular by the next meeting. They all said they'd try.

He'd heard through the grapevine that the West Barton committee were planning a Christmas party at their village hall. It was no secret. So, the East Barton committee had to come up with something special to trump them.

When he'd called Cecilia, she'd taken the opportunity to berate him about being so beastly to Michael. The brigadier had refuted the accusation, saying he had nothing personal against Michael, other than him being the son of his arch-enemy, the *Duchess of Darkness*. Cecilia was not impressed, but the brigadier was not to be swayed on the matter and his veto of their relationship remained in place. Not that Cecilia and Michael let that bother them. They just carried on their relationship secretly, as they had done all summer.

*

At the police station, Sergeant Richards was sat at his desk, also holding a copy of the local newspaper. He'd just known his face would end up on the front pages before long. And, as usual, the press was running the police service down. Dale wasn't sure how they'd managed to get hold of all the stories they'd printed. He really hoped it wasn't someone on the police force that was blabbing. At any rate, someone somewhere certainly had a big mouth.

Dale knew the benighted Best Kept Village Competition wasn't over and that it usually culminated in some sort of winter spectacular. He was hoping, though, that as the winter set in, and the flowers and plants were dying back, there wouldn't be anything horticultural left to vandalise. With any luck, that would be the end of it and he could get back to fighting real crime. He seriously did not want his final years in the police service to be marked by him looking like an inept copper presiding over a total farce.

As autumn turned to winter, the first frosts set in over the Norfolk landscape. Before long, all the trees were bare, the flowers were gone, and all perennial and deciduous plants and shrubs had withered away. In the Bartons, the weather grew colder, greyer and windier. It was thoroughly miserable and most people had only one thing on their mind to cheer them along. The prospect of a festive Christmas – a sentiment that Cynthia Barrington-Smythe was certainly intending to capitalise on.

She chaired the agreed November meeting of the WBBKVC to organise the Christmas Party Extravaganza and, in her habitual domineering fashion, pretty much single-handedly decided on how the event was going to run. She merely needed to delegate the duties to her minions.

Richard was put in charge of sourcing a suitably impressive Christmas tree. He would supply one sustainably from the grounds of the Barton Hall estate. He was also given the task of installing and decorating the tree. Maryam was in charge of decorating the rest of the village hall, including the table decorations, while Vincent was delegated the job of putting up the twinkling fairy lights, both inside and outside the village hall. Michael was entrusted to find some suitable festive CDs for the music system. The hi-fi had a CD multi-changer and could be loaded with five CDs in total, more than enough to last the night. About a third of the village hall floorspace had a parquet dance floor, and once the party was in full swing, the villagers would be encouraged to get up and dance to some of the more popular Christmas hits. Cynthia had put herself in charge of the catering side of things. She was to be ably assisted by Mrs Mei Chen. Mei and her husband, Jin, lived in the village, but ran a Cantonese takeaway in Fakenham. They were kindly going to supply the catering equipment needed for the evening. This consisted of a large electrically heated urn in which they were going to serve the mulled wine. There were also several bain-maries, which would be used to serve a variety of hot canapés and seasonal delicacies. The guest of honour for the evening was going to be the Reverend Clifford Rose. Cynthia had assured him of impartiality, but, nonetheless, she fully intended on using the reverend as her main asset to impress the judge.

Cynthia was very pleased with her plans. The date for the party was set for the 18th December. Doors would open at 7:30pm. Flyers had been produced to advertise the evening and to give all the details of what the villagers could look forward to. The flyers had been posted on the village hall noticeboard, the church noticeboard and even up at the pub. Tickets were to cost a mere £10, with any profits being donated to the church restoration fund – naturally. All they had to do now was gather all the items they needed, then sit back and wait for the days to roll by.

*

The brigadier's plans, on the other hand, were not going quite so well. Mostly because he didn't have any. He was waiting in East Barton village hall for the rest of the committee to turn up for the meeting. Ethel crept in first, took one look at the brigadier's curmudgeonly face and sat down without a word. She knew better than to strike up a conversation when Gerald was in one of his moods. Cecilia came in next. She looked around nervously, drew the same conclusion as Ethel and quickly found a seat. A few other villagers drifted in, interested in what the committee was planning for the Christmas festivities. At this rate, they were going to be severely disappointed. Bernie and Molly were the last to show up and, as they entered the village hall, they were beaming happily. In her hand, Mollie had a copy of the *What's On* guide to Norfolk.

The brigadier looked up grumpily as they drew nearer. 'What are you two so bloody cheerful about?' he grumbled.

'Charming,' said Bernie airily. 'Well, it just so 'appens we've found the solution to our little Christmas problem.'

The brigadier brightened instantly and changed his tone accordingly. 'Really?' he quizzed.

Bernie and Mollie nodded and smiled.

'Well, come on then,' urged the brigadier. 'What have you found? Spill the beans – what!'

Molly thumbed through the *What's On* guide until she found the page she was after. Then, she plonked the magazine down on the table in front of the brigadier. 'Take a look at that,' said Molly.

The brigadier cast his eyes over the advertisement in the magazine and examined the glossy pictures that accompanied it. He began to read aloud for the benefit of everyone in attendance. 'Experience the magic of Lapland right here in Norfolk! Visit Santa in his grotto! See the elves making toys in Santa's workshop! Wonder at the spectacular light show! A festive treat for all the family! Book now to avoid disappointment. Tickets: £15 per person.'

'You see!' exclaimed Bernie. 'It's perfect!'

The brigadier was beaming now, too. 'Well done, you two! You've done a grand job in finding this. It really does look superb!'

'You'd best read the booking conditions,' advised Ethel. 'We don't want any more unpleasant surprises.'

'Quite right, quite right,' agreed the brigadier. He began reading aloud again. 'It says here we need to confirm the numbers and then pay in full online. Once payment has been received, they'll send us the tickets by first-class registered post and a separate letter with detailed directions to the event location. Sounds straightforward enough.'

'We'll need to arrange a minibus,' said Bernie. 'I can get onto that, if you like.'

'Good man,' smiled the brigadier, who was getting back into his stride. 'Now, we better get some flyers drawn up, *tout suite*, and get them up on all the noticeboards. We need to confirm numbers as soon as possible and get this booked. The date for the trip will be set as 18th December. Cecilia, can I rely on you to get the flyers done?'

'Of course, Uncle,' she replied. 'I'll have them done by tomorrow lunchtime.'

'Excellent! Well done, everyone! Let's get on with organising this then and we'll liaise back soon.'

The meeting broke up in considerably better spirits than when it began. The following day, the flyers were posted around the village and in The Barton Arms. Cecilia excelled herself with designing the flyers and the village was soon full of gossip about the impending trip.

A week later, they had the final numbers for how many would be attending the excursion. This consisted of all four committee members, obviously, plus Molly and Bill Rolls. Another nine were coming from the village and, of course, they needed a ticket for the judge. Sixteen in all, which was a pretty decent turnout. Bernie had booked a minibus to arrive at 7:15pm; it would then pick them all up at the village hall and set off at 7:30pm. The brigadier telephoned the North Norfolk Council and informed them of the planned trip. The complimentary ticket for the judge was provided and the brigadier paid for it out of the committee funds. It would be worth the cost when the judge saw the spectacular festive treat they had in store. Confidence was well and truly back in East Barton.

The first few weeks of December flew by and, before they knew it, the big day was fast approaching.

17.

As daylight dawned in West Barton on the 18th December, there was a feeling of palpable excitement hanging in the air. It was going to be one of those bright, cold, crisp winter days, with the sun shining radiantly in a clear blue sky. As the village stirred into life, meticulously calculated plans would soon be falling into place.

At 10am, volunteers began turning up at the village hall to assist with the preparations. Vincent began the unenviable task of untangling the Christmas fairy lights, which had been put away rather carelessly last year. Several villagers were assisting him with the unknotting process while others were checking for blown bulbs and replacing them as necessary.

Maryam was busy setting out the trestle tables and covering them with banqueting roll. The village hall could hold over a hundred people, although realistically they were expecting fifty to sixty. She was laying out enough tables for fifty seats. Anyone else would just have to stand. Besides, they needed a little extra room round the dance floor. Her assistants were starting to lay out the Christmas decorations, tinsel and table centrepieces.

Mai Chen was making a start on the catering. Some of the sturdier OAPs in the village had lent her a hand by bringing in the large urn and the bain-maries from her car. The big urn was set in place on the kitchen serving hatch. It was filled with red wine and the herbs and spices needed for the mulling process. In order to heat it up, all that was required was for the urn to be plugged in and switched on about half an hour before serving.

Cynthia herself was overseeing the food preparation. At the moment, they were making the cold appetisers that would go into the fridge on platters, ready to go out on the buffet table later. The village hall had basic kitchen facilities. A large fridge and freezer, an oven, and a sink for washing up. It was adequate for a buffet, but Mrs Chen's catering equipment would make things a lot easier to serve the hot food and drink.

Richard had spent the morning scouring the estate for a suitable Christmas tree with his groundsmen. They'd finally located a fine specimen in a copse at the extremity of his grounds, which was duly felled. Richard arrived at the village hall at around 11:30am with the tree strapped to the top of his 4x4. He'd had the sense to bring his groundsman with him to help install the tree in the hall. It was a little larger than necessary and they'd had some difficulty dragging it through the entrance door. Pine needles had flown everywhere, which Cynthia had tutted and fussed about, but eventually they had it installed and she had to acknowledge that it looked rather splendid.

Cynthia allowed the volunteers an hour's break for lunch, but insisted everyone needed to return at 1pm to finish the set-up.

An hour later, everyone began to drift back into the village hall. Michael put in an appearance and entered the hall, carrying a large cardboard box.

'What on earth have you got in there?' Cynthia challenged him.

'I've just been into town to see a friend who runs a mobile disco. He's let me borrow some gear,' explained Michael. He opened the box and lifted out two sets of multicoloured disco lights, a mirrored glitter ball and a small machine that threw out a surprising array of laser light patterns.

'That's a bit high-tech for a village Christmas party, isn't it?' queried Cynthia.

'Don't worry, Mum. I won't switch them on until well into the night,' he assured her.

Satisfied, she gave him a rare smile and resumed her catering duties. They were preparing the hot canapés now and laying them out on baking trays, ready to pop in the oven later on. They'd then be transferred to the bain-maries to keep warm. Cynthia and Mai would need to come in half an hour before the doors opened to put everything in the oven and switch on the urn and bain-maries.

Under Cynthia's watchful eye, the decorations were completed and the fairy lights were all set up, inside and out. The majestic Christmas tree was festooned in glittering baubles and was looking very impressive. The village hall had been transformed into a utopia of cheery and festive Christmas bliss. It had gone dark outside, so they were able to test the full effect of the exterior lighting. Vincent had excelled himself and the village hall was glimmering and glowing with hundreds of twinkling fairy lights. They turned them off again, for now.

Cynthia was finally content that everything was ready. It was nearly 5pm, so she called it a day and let everyone go home to get themselves ready for the evening's festivities. She'd arranged with Mrs Chen to reconvene at 7pm at the village hall, with everyone else to follow at 7:30pm.

*

Under the cover of darkness and concealed in some nearby bushes, a figure dressed all in black had been watching the proceedings at West Barton village hall for the last ten minutes or so. Everyone had just left the village hall to return to their respective homes. Even so, the figure waited an extra ten minutes to be sure no one else was loitering inside.

Moments later, a hand wearing a Lincoln-green glove tried the latch on the back door of the village hall. It wasn't locked. The door led directly into the kitchen. Stealing inside, the intruder looked around the small kitchen and spied the item it was looking for, sitting on the serving hatch. The metal lid of the large urn was removed and the gloved hand delved into its jacket pocket and reappeared holding a small jar of pills. On the jar was a label with a round yellow smiley face emblazoned upon it. The lid of the jar was unscrewed and the entire contents of the jar were poured into the urn full of mulled wine. The empty jar was pocketed again and the lid of the urn replaced.

The figure then noiselessly crossed the room and switched on the hi-fi. The CD multi-changer was ejected and the third Christmas compilation CD was removed and replaced with an altogether different compilation. The multi-changer was then reinserted and the hi-fi was switched off again.

Leaving the same way it had come in, the figure carefully closed the back door and made off back into the darkness.

*

The tickets for the Lapland trip had arrived promptly about a week ago, delivered by registered post. Along with the tickets, an envelope containing the directions to the venue was delivered at the same time. The brigadier had counted the tickets before he allowed the postman to leave. There were sixteen, so all was in order.

The brigadier had arranged with all those attending the trip to meet in East Barton village hall by 7:15pm to await the minibus. Everyone, including the Best Kept

Village judge, was now sat patiently waiting for the minibus to arrive. They heard it pull up outside, bang on time. The brigadier got up and went outside to talk to the driver.

'Evening, squire,' called the driver chirpily as he got out from the driver's side. 'And a very merry Christmas to you!'

'Thank you,' responded the brigadier, 'and a merry Christmas to you, too – what!'

Ready in his hand, the brigadier waved the envelope containing the directions under the driver's nose. 'Here's the address of where we need to go.'

'Thank you, squire,' said the driver, taking the envelope and placing it on the dashboard. He turned back to the brigadier. 'Do you mind if I use your loo before we set off? Me back teeth are floating.'

'Oh, well, I suppose so,' said the brigadier, giving him an unsavoury glance. 'It's this way. Follow me.' He led the driver into the village hall, pointed out where the loo was located and then sat down again to wait.

*

Outside East Barton village hall, a figure clad in black was hiding behind the wheelie bins at the side of the hall. The figure had been waiting for an opportunity like this and, seizing the moment, sneaked out from behind the bins and sidled over to the driver's door of the minibus.

Reaching inside, a navy-blue gloved hand picked

up the envelope containing the directions and stuffed it quickly away in a pocket. The figure then produced a similar-looking envelope from the inside of its jacket and placed it on the dashboard instead. The figure then returned swiftly to its hiding place behind the wheelie bins before anyone could notice and waited until the coast was clear.

*

A minute or two later, the minibus driver stepped back out of the entrance door of the village hall, followed by the brigadier, the judge, the East Barton committee and everyone else attending the evening's excursion.

The driver opened the sliding side door of the minibus and helped all his passengers inside. When everyone was on board, he returned to the driver's seat and reached for the envelope. Opening it, he read the address and punched the postcode into his satnav.

'We're all off to Lapland then?' he asked cheerily.

'That's right, my good man,' replied the brigadier. 'Drive on!'

The driver raised an eyebrow. *Mine's not to reason why*, he thought to himself. *I'm just the driver.* He put the minibus into gear and off they went.

Bernie and Molly got the festivities started by getting everyone singing along to the good old Christmas song 'Jingle Bell Rock' as they made their way merrily out of the village. Once they'd gone, a dark figure emerged from behind the village hall bins and faded into the night.

18.

At 7pm, Cynthia met Mai back at the village hall and between them they set about finalising the catering. The big urn containing the mulled wine was switched on to heat up, as was the oven to preheat. While they waited, Cynthia went round switching all the festive lights on, both inside and out, so that when folk arrived, they'd have maximum impact.

Just then, the front door of the hall burst open suddenly and Lord Braithwaite reeled in. 'What-ho!' he greeted them.

'Richard, it doesn't start until 7:30pm,' tutted Cynthia. 'What are you doing here already?' She thought she could detect a slight whiff of malt whisky emanating from his vicinity.

'I thought I'd come to lend a hand. Is the bar open?' he asked with a slight slur.

'No, it isn't, so just behave! Mrs Chen and I are still finishing cooking the hot food,' she reprimanded him.

She turned to Mai and asked, 'How are the Christmas puddings coming along?'

'They've been steaming since 5pm this afternoon,' replied Mai.

'What a coincidence! So have I!' quipped Richard.

'That's quite enough of that!' scolded Cynthia. 'Now, make yourself useful and take the hot canapés out of the oven and put them in the bain-maries.'

'Oh, very well,' he said, looking chastised.

'And mind you stay away from the judge when she arrives. I don't want you breathing fumes all over her!'

Richard pulled a face behind her back, but did as he was told.

Cynthia laid out the cold appetisers for the buffet, while Richard and Mai filled the bain-maries with the hot canapés and Christmas puds. All the food was then ready.

At 7:25pm, Cynthia turned the hi-fi on and pressed the button for the first Christmas CD to start playing. The music added the final touch to create the perfect festive atmosphere.

Shortly after, people begin to steadily drift in and soon the village hall was filling up nicely. The Best Kept Village judge made an entrance a few minutes later, clipboard in hand. She nodded cordially to Cynthia, who wished her a happy Christmas and offered her a glass of mulled wine. The judge was teetotal, so requested a fruit juice instead. Cynthia smiled sweetly and went off to fetch it for her. But under her breath, she was cursing her. She'd hoped to soften the judge up a bit with a few mulled wines. Never mind. Cynthia had certainly helped herself to one, though, while she was up at the servery. She'd noticed Richard was knocking them back all right. The man was incorrigible.

Reverend Rose was one of the next to arrive. He stepped warily through the entrance door, guitar in hand, trying to spy the quickest route to the bar, when he was immediately collared by Cynthia.

'Oh, Reverend,' she cooed, ensuring the judge heard every word. 'How very *community-spirited* of you to stop by for our little village party. I had no idea you were going to pop in.'

'But didn't you specifically—' he began.

'*And* you've brought your guitar,' she said, quickly cutting him off. 'I do hope you'll be playing some seasonal songs for us.' *If this doesn't get us a few extra points*, she pondered, *then nothing will.*

'I'd be happy to.' He smiled cheerfully, then bid her a merry Christmas and made his way over to the servery, where Richard thrust a glass of mulled wine into his hand.

'Get that down you, Vicar,' he blared. 'Bottoms up!'

The reverend took a sip and smiled weakly at Lord Braithwaite. He was mightily relieved when Michael came over to chat to him instead.

The party was going with a swing. The mulled wine was proving a hit and was going down rapidly. Cynthia tapped a teaspoon against a glass and announced the buffet was open. Everyone descended eagerly to sample the festive culinary delights. While people were readily tucking in, Reverend Rose kindly went over to stand on the dance floor and played several Christmas songs on his guitar. The villagers sung along with him. It was a heart-warming moment. Cynthia was delighted it was all going so well. As she took in the picture-perfect festive gathering taking place around her, she was even beginning to experience strange feelings of ecstatic warmth and euphoria.

*

The minibus had been on the road for the best part of fifty-five minutes. Bernie and Molly's repertoire of Christmas songs had run dry ten minutes ago. The brigadier was getting a bit restless. He'd thought the venue was a bit closer to home than this.

'I say,' he said to the driver, 'are we nearly there yet?'

'Not long now, squire,' replied the driver. 'Five or six more miles.'

It seemed to the brigadier that they were heading for Great Yarmouth. It made sense, he supposed. It was a big cheesy tourist resort – just the sort of place you'd expect a Christmas theme park to be set up.

Sure enough, the driver took the next exit off the dual carriageway and they headed down into Great Yarmouth. They were almost at the seafront when the driver turned right down a smaller street and then turned left into a large car park. Sure enough, there was a large blue neon sign flashing 'Lapland' on and off above a canopied entrance. The brigadier had been expecting a slightly more dazzling array of Christmas lights if he were being totally honest. But he hid his disappointment and pressed on. Perhaps the display was better once you were inside.

'Onward, troops!' he hollered cheerfully and ushered the group out of the minibus and towards the entrance.

The driver was scheduled to pick them up again at 11pm, so he got back in the minibus and set off in search of somewhere he could get a good meal to pass the time. He drove out of the car park and headed towards the seafront. Turning right along the main seafront promenade, his route took him past the front façade of 'Lapland'. Here, there was a vastly larger flashing neon sign, which read:

Lapland
Norfolk's Most Exotic
Lap Dancing & Striptease Club

The driver gave a saucy chuckle to himself. He found it incredulous that the group of old codgers that'd hired him were having a night out in there. No wonder they'd given him the address in a discreet envelope. He shook his head in disbelief and drove off further along the seafront.

The brigadier and his group reached the canopied entrance, where they were confronted with a tin sign tacked to a sturdy wooden door. The sign read: 'Main Entrance at Front of Building. This Entrance for VIP Prepaid Tickets ONLY.'

Well, the brigadier wasn't sure they were VIPs exactly, but they had definitely prepaid their tickets. There was only one way to find out, so the brigadier gave a sharp rap on the door. They waited a while, but there was no reply. He tried the handle and found the door was unlocked. He pushed it wide open and marched brusquely inside, the others following in his wake.

They found themselves in a tastefully decorated lobby area. The low-level lighting emitted hues in shades of pink and purple, while the soft furnishings were sumptuous velvet and suede. There was a large chaise longue along one wall and next to it was a small desk with a bell-ring. There were also plush cloakrooms located along the back wall. Down one side of the lobby, a wide corridor led off to the right-hand side. There were several rooms located down the corridor. Luxurious purple velvet drapes covered the entrances to these rooms. Another wide corridor led off to the left-hand side, but it was hard to see where this led due to the dim lighting.

The brigadier was baffled that there was no one about to take their tickets. *This is a rum place*, he thought. *No doubt about it.* He was beginning to get irritated by the lack of customer service, so he walked over to the bell-ring and gave it a ping. Again, there was no response. He turned to the group, who were all looking at him expectantly.

'Right,' said the brigadier, starting to get fired up. 'I'm going to go and see if I can find someone in charge. I suggest you all split up and try, too. We'll meet up again once we get someone's attention.' With that, he marched off purposefully down the right-hand corridor, searching for any signs of life. The rest of the group stood looking at one another for a while, wondering what to do next.

Bernie and Molly caught each other's eye and mutually decided to act.

'This way,' called Bernie and led the way down the left-hand corridor. All but Bill followed him. Bill thought the brigadier shouldn't be left on his own, so he loped off down the right-hand corridor after him.

Halfway along the left-hand corridor, Bernie and Molly's group encountered another smaller corridor that led off to the right. Molly, Ethel and Cecilia broke off from the main group to investigate where it led. Bernie and the remaining group carried on to the end of the larger corridor, where they came upon a huge, grand sweeping staircase that wound down to a lower level. There was a sign on the wall that read: 'To the Main Auditorium' and they could definitely hear sounds of life rising from the floor below. As they went down the stairs, they could see the entrance to the auditorium. Above it was a blue neon sign that read: 'The Grotto.' Finally, they were getting somewhere.

*

Michael was delighted his CD compilation was going down so well. While the first CD compilation had been quite mellow, he'd intentionally tried to ramp up the tempo of the second CD compilation with some of the more rhythmical Christmas pop songs, in the hope it might entice one or two villagers onto the dance floor. Well, he needn't have worried because there were at least twenty people on the dance floor now, albeit doing some fairly lame dancing, but nonetheless he was really pleased. He caught his mother's eye and she smiled warmly at him and gave him the thumbs up, which was an unusual gesture for her to make. She must be in a very good mood, he surmised.

Cynthia *was* in a good mood. She'd seldom felt this good. The party was really getting going. She'd sneaked a peek at the judge's clipboard a little while ago and she'd given them top marks so far. Excellent news.

A new festive pop song started on the hi-fi. She'd never noticed what a good song it was before. She even started tapping her foot in time to the music. Reverend Rose had just been dragged up onto the dance floor by some of the more exuberant elderly ladies in the village and they all began bopping away. Cynthia felt an overwhelming urge to get up and join them. She saw Richard, Maryam and Vincent were already up there. *What the hell*, she thought. She was damn well going to. She strode purposefully onto the dance floor next to the vicar and joined the fray.

Michael's jaw nearly hit the floor when he saw his mother go up to dance. He'd never seen her do anything like that in his entire life. Mind you, this music was truly magic. He, too, was experiencing a great desire to get up there and revel in the fun.

The current song, the last one on CD 2, came to an end and there was a disappointed groan from the crowd on the dance floor, who were eager for more. After a little whirring, the CD multi-changer automatically switched onto the next disc, CD 3.

The dance music that started was like nothing any of them had heard before. There was an incredible booming bass that seemed to resonate with the soul, and the fast-paced hypnotic drumbeats and synthesised rhythms were providing a musical experience that was pummelling their senses. For a moment, everyone just stood still and listened, not comprehending entirely what they were hearing. Michael took the opportunity to switch the whole array of disco lights on. Suddenly, the revellers came to life almost as one. And all hell broke loose.

Lord Braithwaite, who'd had way more than his fair share of mulled wine, was the first to react. He knew all about this kind of music. He'd been on a trip to New York once and had seen some teenagers performing in the street to this kind of thing. Breakdancing was what it was called.

'Stand aside,' he ordered loudly. 'Watch and learn!'

In his mind, he had every intention of performing a graceful forward somersault to land neatly onto the dance floor. He allowed himself a small run-up and, with arms outstretched, he launched himself into the air. He made it about halfway through the mid-air turn, but then gravity decided to make its presence felt. He crashed into the centre of the dance floor, landing flat on his back. Unperturbed, he grasped his knees to his chest and attempted a dazzlingly rapid spinning manoeuvre. He ran out of steam pretty quickly, so Vincent assisted him by grabbing him by his shoes and shoving him round and round. The appreciative crowd whooped loudly and gave him a round of applause.

'And that's what you call breakdancing!' he shouted triumphantly from the ground – which, in his case, held an element of truth. He'd just fractured two of his ribs.

*

The brigadier was making his way down the wide corridor, passing the rooms with the heavy purple drapes covering the entrances. Before long, he reached the end of the corridor and had to double back on himself. He decided to try the chamber nearest to him, so he drew the curtain back a bit and poked his head round the side to peer inside.

'I'm looking for someone in charge,' he proclaimed loudly into the void.

There was no reply, so he carried on inside. The room was obviously some sort of study. Probably the manager's office, by the look of it. The room had the same low lighting as in the lobby. There were floor-to-ceiling bookcases all around the walls and a large leather-top desk at the far end. Beside the desk, there was a small console table with a selection of decanters holding a variety of liquors.

'Hallo!' said the brigadier sternly again. 'I need someone in authority!'

There came a faint noise from the shadows to his left. 'I may be able to help you with that,' came a sultry voice from the darkness. Hidden in the dim light was an old-fashioned wing-backed armchair. A lady was sitting in the chair and now rose slowly to her feet and came forward into view to greet the brigadier.

The brigadier could see she clearly held a position of great importance in the corporation, although he did think dressing in the style of a headmistress was pushing it a bit far. She wore a black cloak over her suit and had an old-school mortar board perched neatly over her immaculately coiffured hair. The heels on her stilettos were the highest he'd ever seen. In her hand, she held a sturdy walking cane with a curved handle.

'I'm Brigadier Faraday,' he introduced himself and proffered his hand.

She took his hand in hers and gave it a gentle squeeze. 'There's no need to be so formal,' she chided him softly. 'What's your first name?'

'Er, Gerald,' he replied. 'And you are, Madam…?'

'Swish,' she said softly. 'Natasha Swish.'

The brigadier wasn't sure if it was his imagination, but he seemed to be getting rather hot all of a sudden.

'Madam Swish, I can't tell you how happy I am to find someone in authority,' he announced. 'Shall we get straight down to business?'

'All in good time, Gerald,' she murmured. 'Why

don't you pour yourself a drink while I take your coat. There's a fine brandy in the decanter.'

The brigadier was rather partial to a good brandy. He was also enjoying the attention he was receiving from the charming Madam Swish. While she took his coat, she indicated the drinks table. 'Do help yourself.' She smiled encouragingly.

'Most kind,' said the brigadier politely.

While Natasha went to hang his coat over a chair, the brigadier walked over to the console table and bent over to inspect the decanters. He selected the one containing brandy, removed the crystal stopper and poured himself a generous measure. He leant over further to savour the aroma.

'Ah, yes, a fine vintage,' he said happily.

Behind him, Natasha had returned and was carefully flexing her cane between her fingers. She took careful aim.

As the brigadier took a sip of the brandy, he heard an odd whooshing sound, followed by a dull thwack. And then, he felt a sensation as though someone had placed a white-hot wire across his backside. The brandy was expelled from his mouth in a cloud of vapour.

'*What the bloody blues blazes!*' he managed to splutter, his face turning a crimson shade of red.

'You've been a very naughty boy,' Madam Swish told him sternly.

'I most certainly have not!' he protested hotly.

'And Santa doesn't bring any toys to naughty boys,' she continued.

'*Santa!* Bloody Satan, more like! What do you think you're playing at?' he bellowed.

Whoosh! Thwack! And his buttocks were on fire again.

'Madam, will you kindly desist?!' he roared in pain.

But he wasn't hanging round for an answer. He was off like a whippet out of a trap. As he scrambled across the room, grabbing his coat off the chair, he lost his footing for a split second and fell to his hands and knees. Natasha didn't miss the opportunity to give him a third lashing as he tried to regain his feet. The pain was excruciating and he howled in agony. He shot off again and, hastily shoving the drapes aside, he fled down the corridor back towards the lobby.

'Oi!' shrieked Natasha after him. 'Come back here! You haven't paid!' She set off after him, tottering about a little in her high heeled stilettos.

Back in the lobby, the brigadier spied the cloakrooms and pelted full speed into the gents. He should be safe in here, he calculated.

Natasha had seen him duck into the cloakroom. *You don't get away that easily, you old devil*, she mused. She sat down on the chaise longue and waited for him to re-emerge. Extracting a file from her pocket, she began to shape her nails. She was in no rush.

The brigadier stood in one of the cubicles and locked the door, desperately trying to think of a way he could escape from the clutches of Madam Swish.

*

The cheers and applause from Richard's antics were starting to subside. Cynthia had watched his performance with interest and thought that while he'd certainly shown great enthusiasm, he had lacked certain other qualities. Such as any skill or coordination, for instance. She decided she could do much better. She had seen some of Michael's music videos over the last year or so and recalled one in particular where the dancers were pretending to be robots. Well, she could do that all right. It'd be a piece of cake. She walked to the centre of the dance floor and, shoving some of the elderly folk firmly out of her way, she cleared some space around her.

She set her face like stone and stared blankly ahead in what she thought was a robotic nature. The dance music was still booming and she began to move her head from side to side in quick jerky motions. Next, she lifted her arms out in front of her, elbows bent and hands outstretched. She performed the same rapid jerking motions. She repeated the process with her hips and finally her legs, until her whole body was in motion. She then pretended to stack some imaginary boxes. The effect was surprisingly good, and she was getting cheered and egged on by the crowd. She was loving it. It was harder work than she'd anticipated, though. She was calling into action muscles and tendons that she'd previously never known she possessed. Although the newly discovered parts of her body responded well, they were soon beginning to tire and ache. But Cynthia was on a roll, so she ignored the fact her body was imploring her to stop and carried on her highly energetic cyber dancing.

Maryam was getting jealous of the attention Richard and Cynthia were enjoying. She was keen to show everyone what she could do. She'd picked up a few tricks of her own while she'd been at medical college. She'd joined a club at university where she'd learnt disco and pop dancing, and some other funky moves that were popular at the time.

At the edge of the dance floor, she removed her shoes and chucked them roughly in the direction of where she thought her husband was sitting. Her aim was slightly askew, however, as they regrettably landed in the lap of the Best Kept Village judge. The judge was already starting to be appalled at the turn of events that were unfolding before her eyes and the arrival of someone's shoes landing in her lap didn't help matters.

Maryam took to the floor in her stockinged feet and began an intriguing dance move where she appeared to be walking on the spot. And then, to everyone's amazement, although she continued the walking forward motion, she actually started sliding backwards across the floor. The crowd hollered in admiration.

Even Cynthia paused her robotics for an instant and watched Maryam glissade past her, *moonwalking* backwards across the floor. When she reached the edge of the dance floor, she spun round sharply, uttering a high-pitched 'Oooh!', punched a fist in the air and began sliding back the opposite way. The whole village hall erupted in cheers and clapped enthusiastically at the great entertainment being provided for them.

Not to be outdone, Vincent was up next. The only

dance-related memory he possessed was when, as a teenager, his elder sister had dragged him along to the cinema to watch some ghastly American chick-flick movie about disco dancing. He couldn't remember the name of the film, but he could vaguely remember some of the dancing sequences. They all looked fairly straightforward, as he recalled.

Vincent was dressed in his habitual ill-fitting black suit and as he strutted onto the dance floor, he removed his jacket, revealing a stark white shirt and black waistcoat he wore underneath. He started twirling the jacket round and round above his head, while he held the other hand to his waist and began revolving his hips, in what he imagined was a highly provocative style. He was getting some wolf whistles and catcalls from some of the elderly – and almost certainly poor-sighted – ladies in the room. Vincent's mouth broke into a crooked grin. He let his jacket fly into the crowd, where it fluttered in the air momentarily before settling gracefully over the judge's head. She screamed in horror.

Striking a dramatic pose with his arm and index finger pointing in the air, he slanted his leg to one side in a rakish posture and continued his pelvic thrusts. In his mind, he was exactly replicating the disco moves he'd seen all those years ago. In reality, he looked more like *Riff Raff* doing the *Time Warp*. Either way, he was severely overdoing the hip movements and presently he felt something give way in the area of his nether regions. He collapsed to the ground, clutching his crotch, and thrashed around on the dance floor, rolling from side to side. Everyone assumed it was some provocative part of his act and instead of helping him or calling a doctor, they gave him a rousing cheer and a standing ovation.

*

Bill had tried to catch up with the brigadier, following in his tracks, but by the time he'd made his way across the lobby, the brigadier was nowhere to be seen. Bill was standing close to the first chamber down the wide corridor. His legs were giving him gyp as usual and he needed to sit down. He went up to the purple velvet drape that covered the entrance and pushed it aside. He walked unsteadily into the low-lit room and stopped in his tracks. Against the wall at the far end of the room, there was a large comfy sofa. And sat on the sofa were three pretty elves, chatting among themselves. Halfway along the right-hand wall, there was a large glass display cabinet, full of items of merchandise. On the left side, there was a console table with a variety of drink bottles set upon it. There was nothing else in the room. As Bill stepped in, the three elves stopped chatting and all turned to look at him. They all smiled sweetly at him.

'Hello,' they all said at once.

'Oh, hello. I'm sorry ter bother you, but I'm lookin' for somewhere I can have a proper sit down, if yer know wha' I mean,' said Bill shyly. 'Are you Santa's elves, then?'

'Oh, yes,' said the elf in the middle. She had blonde hair poking out from under her red-and-green striped floppy hat. 'My name's Fi-Fi.'

'I'm Candy,' said the elf with brown hair, giving him a wink.

'And I'm Bella,' said the elf with red hair, blowing him a kiss. 'What's your name?'

'I'm Bill. Nice ter meet yer.'

Fi-Fi stood up from the sofa and, seeing he was a little unsteady on his feet, came over and held his arm. 'Won't you come and sit down with us?' she implored, tugging at his arm.

'That'd be nice,' said Bill, beaming. These elves were certainly very friendly.

On the way to the sofa, they passed the glass display cabinet and Bill stopped to peer inside. 'Wow-wee,' he remarked. 'Just look at all them toy space rockets!'

'I've never heard them called that before,' said Fi-Fi, giggling.

'Do you make all the toys here in the workshop, then?' asked Bill innocently.

'No, silly!' chided Fi-Fi playfully. 'They come from Sweden, I think.'

Bill gave this some thought. 'I think you mean the North Pole,' he suggested.

Fi-Fi looked baffled for a second, then shrugged and laughed, and continued leading him to the sofa. 'Now, you sit here, Bill, between Candy and Bella, and I'll get you a drink. How about a lovely glass of rum?'

'That'd be nice,' nodded Bill amiably.

While Fi-Fi went to fix him his drink, Candy and Bella sidled up closer to him on the sofa, smiling and giggling all the while. Bill was grinning like a Cheshire cat.

Fi-Fi returned with the rum and handed the glass to Bill, who grasped the drink with a shaky hand and took a large gulp. 'Thank you,' he smiled happily.

'Do you like our costumes, Bill?' she asked suggestively. 'I can give you a twirl, if you like.'

Bill nodded enthusiastically. Fi-Fi pirouetted round on her tiptoes so Bill could see her whole outfit properly. 'I like yer pom-pom,' he said, pointing at her lower back.

Each of the elves had a white pom-pom about the size of a grapefruit fastened onto their outfits with a press stud. They were designed to be easily removed.

'I bet you do, you cheeky thing!' she said sassily. 'It comes off, you know...'

'Does it?' he said with a quavering voice.

She leant over a little and wiggled her derriere at him, so that the pom-pom jiggled about. 'You can take it off, if you'd like,' she said lasciviously.

Bill started to raise a trembling hand.

She craned her head over her shoulder so she could look at him and then gave him a saucy smile. 'Why don't you use your teeth, tiger?' she purred raunchily.

'Oh right,' he sighed breathlessly. 'If you say so, Fi-Fi.'

He put his drink down and then raised his right hand to his mouth. With a soft squelching sound, Bill removed his dentures and brandished them in his hand with a gummy smile. Holding his gnashers like a pair of castanets, he then made a lunge for Fi-Fi's pom-pom.

Observing the gruesome spectacle going on behind her, Fi-Fi screamed loudly and shot off across the room to avoid the incoming toothy assault. Horrified, Candy and Bella quickly followed suit and ran off through the curtains after Fi-Fi.

Bill looked crestfallen and was perplexed to know what he'd done wrong. 'Whatsha matter?' he cried after them. 'You told me ter use me teesh!' He hurriedly cast his dentures aside on the sofa and hobbled off after the elves as fast as he could.

*

Reverend Rose was observing the antics being performed on the dance floor with a highly critical eye. In his opinion, as a trained musician, they were all a bunch of amateur shysters. This wasn't what real music was about. He'd show them what a proper rock and roller could do.

Grabbing his guitar as he rose to his feet, he first made a slight detour into the kitchenette, where Mrs Chen was busy washing up. Before she had time to protest, he'd purloined one of her best red tea towels and tied it tightly round his forehead in the time-honoured fashion of an aging rock star.

Giving her a cursory nod, he burst out of the kitchenette and jogged to the edge of dance floor, where he fell to his knees and slid across the parquet floor, thrashing out some power chords along the way. Egged on by tumultuous applause, he regained his feet and proceeded to headbang his way around the dance floor in a most alarming way.

The reverend was a big fan of heavy rock, although – given his position in the church – he'd had to keep it largely under wraps. In his mind, he was seeking inspiration on how to perform the perfect finale to his improvised routine. He'd never really understood why some rockers smashed their guitars up at the end of a gig, but now it was all crystal clear to him. Once you'd performed the perfect show, there was no more need for the instruments. So, they had to be sacrificed. It was obvious to him now.

He looked maniacally around the room, searching for the ideal receptacle on which to carry out the deed. His eyes fell upon Mrs Chen's large metal urn containing the mulled wine. *Perfect*, he thought. He air-guitared his way over to the serving hatch and then hoisted his beloved guitar above his head. He paused momentarily and then brought it crashing down onto the top of the urn with an ear-splitting clang. The urn buckled under the blow, but the guitar stayed in shape. The reverend decided to give it more welly and began beating the urn relentlessly with the guitar.

Disturbed by the racket, Mrs Chen's head appeared round the side of the kitchenette door and was startled to see the cause of the commotion. She ducked back into the kitchenette and re-emerged armed with a straw broom.

'What are you doing to my urn, crazy priest?' she yelled at the reverend and began whacking him unceremoniously with the broom.

The vicar barely noticed and continued his brutal assault on the urn. With one last mighty blow, the guitar finally splintered into pieces. The crowd roared its approval. The urn fared no better and split in two, showering everyone in the vicinity with warm red liquid – the judge taking the brunt of the splattering. It was like a scene from a demonic exorcism. The reverend stood panting for a moment, drenched in steaming red wine, and then passed out.

The Best Kept Village judge was at the end of her tether. She'd had enough. Daubed in mulled wine from head to foot, she snatched up her clipboard and ran for the exit. If the West Barton committee thought this extraordinary spectacle was going to impress her, they had another thing coming. She'd never seen such a display of wanton decadence. In her opinion, it was worse than Sodom and Gomorrah. She'd certainly be giving them some very poor marks.

*

The narrow corridor that Ethel, Cecilia and Molly were exploring turned left and then right again, before finally leading them to a small waiting hall. There were several comfortable-looking seats scattered around the area and in one of them was seated an attractive young lady reading a magazine.

Intriguingly, at the back of the hall, there was a circular opening in the floor, in the centre of which was located what looked like a fireman's pole. One end was fixed to the ceiling, while the other end went down through the hole.

There was a sign on the back wall that read: 'To The Grotto' and an arrow pointing down towards the hole. Next to the sign were two lights, positioned like a mini traffic light. One red light and, below that, a green light. Currently, the red light was glowing.

Ethel noticed that the young lady who was sat waiting was still in her school uniform. She looked a little old to still be in school, but it was amazing what these girls could do with the right make-up. Ethel considered the schoolgirl's skirt to be awfully short, but she knew only too well that was how the young girls liked to present themselves nowadays.

'You'll catch your death of cold dressed like that,' Ethel informed her. 'Don't you have an anorak?'

The girl just rolled her eyes in response.

Just then, the lights changed and the green light came on. The schoolgirl stood up.

'Excuse me,' she said nonchalantly and walked over to the pole. She grasped hold with both hands and, wrapping her legs firmly round it, slowly slid down the pole and disappeared into the hole. The light turned red again.

'Well, that's mighty odd,' observed Molly.

The others agreed.

'Still, it looks like a fun way for folk to get down to Santa's grotto,' said Cecilia.

As if to concur, there was a big cheer from somewhere below them.

'Sounds like they're having a blast down there,' agreed Ethel.

'I don't much like poles,' said Molly. 'I wonder if there's another way down.'

'Och, don't be such a wet weekend,' scolded Ethel. 'It's just a wee bit of fun.'

Ethel was being uncharacteristically joyful, thought Molly.

'Anyway, I can't see any other way down,' Cecilia noted. 'We'll have to go this way.'

'Well, you can go first,' said Molly firmly.

They sat down in the chairs and patiently waited their turn. Soon enough, the light turned green.

'Come on then, girls,' said Cecilia cheerfully. 'Santa's waiting!'

She stood and led the way to the pole. Copying the technique of the schoolgirl, Cecilia grabbed the pole and began to slide down. Ethel followed closely behind. Molly hesitated for a moment, but when she saw the others had disappeared through the floor, she plucked up the courage and hurled herself at the pole, holding on for dear life.

The pole had not been designed to take the weight of three people. Nor had it been designed with a seventeen-stone farmer's wife in mind. These factors coupled together meant that the pole began to wobble precariously and started to give way. The metal was buckling in the middle and the bolts securing it to the ceiling sheared off altogether.

Cecilia reached the bottom and gracefully stepped off the pole and onto the floor. There were bright stage lights shining up into her face so she couldn't see a thing, but she could definitely hear the roar of applause from a large audience. Ethel alighted next, to slightly less rapturous applause and with a modicum of confusion from the crowd. She looked around, completely baffled, but could see nothing either.

With a terrible groaning noise and a sound of tortured metal, the pole ultimately gave way. It slowly began to bend, with Molly still clinging on desperately to the top end, shrieking like a banshee. It gradually bent double and then deposited her abruptly onto the centre of the stage, flat on her back and with legs akimbo. Her arms were still wrapped firmly round the pole. The crowd went wild.

Watching the show from the auditorium floor, Dai Williams gave a hearty cheer and applauded loudly. Dai was enjoying a night out with the rest of his teammates from the Aberystwyth Rugby Club. They'd won their match against Great Yarmouth that afternoon and were in top form. They'd had a few pints and a slap-up meal in town before heading along to the Lapland Club for the Christmas show. They were enjoying the evening. The last act, the naughty schoolgirl, had been the best so far and he was watching the next one in great anticipation.

The first girl down the pole was a stunner, but the two that followed had him slightly perplexed. That said, he had to admit the special effects with the collapsing pole were really impressive. He saw now that the pretty girl was looking round for a way off the stage towards the back. However, the vision in tartan, with a face like a grumpy gorilla, was approaching the side of the stage nearest him. Dai took some money from his wallet and, with his curiosity piqued, he made his way over to her.

Ethel realised that not only were they not in Santa's grotto, but they seemed to be on a stage in front of a huge and boisterous crowd. She needed to find a way off the stage as quickly as possible. She walked over to the edge and was looking down to see if she could find a way off, when she was accosted by a slovenly-looking ruffian. For some reason that she couldn't fathom, he was waving a five-pound note at her.

'What do you think you're doing with that?' she asked him gruffly.

'Well,' Dai replied with a cheeky grin, 'I was going to snap it into your knicker elastic.'

Ethel's mouth fell open in shock. 'You'll be doing no such thing!' she retorted. 'You filthy beast!' And with that, she gave him a swipe across the head with her sturdy handbag.

The baked bean tin concealed inside connected soundly with Dai's temple. The blow sent him reeling, half unconscious, across the auditorium floor and into a table full of lads out on a stag do. They'd just bought a round of drinks with chasers, which had cost them a small fortune. Dai flew into the table and knocked the lot over and straight into their laps, soaking them from the waist down.

'Sorry, boys,' Dai managed to say before slumping to the floor.

The lads were none too impressed. As a group they

got to their feet and hauled Dai up by the scruff of his neck. Grabbing a limb each they then bodily threw him back towards the tables where the Aberystwyth 1st XV were sitting.

Poor Dai went whirling across the floor again and straight into his team-mates. About ten pints of lager went flying into the air and a dozen of the Welshmen were knocked over like bowling pins. Inevitably they disturbed other tables, and more and more drinks were going over. Within thirty seconds there was a full-scale bar brawl going on.

The Welshmen, accustomed to this sort of thing occurring on the playing field, instinctively formed themselves into an impromptu ruck and had burst into their war song 'Men of Harlech.' They were ready for battle!

Cecilia had managed to get off the stage using some steps she'd discovered at the back. She was making her way across the auditorium when the carnage ensued. She froze in terror as the violence broke out. She was standing next to the Welshmen and seeing her plight, they beckoned her over and offered their protection, which she gratefully accepted.

Molly had finally relinquished her grip on the pole and was unsteadily getting back to her feet. She looked around for the others but couldn't see them. As she neared the edge of the stage, she could see the whole auditorium was in riot. Close by, she saw Cecilia looking terrified and then being dragged into a group of huge thuggish looking men. She burst into action.

'Don't worry Cecilia,' she bawled across the room. 'I'm coming!'

The Welshmen were observing her actions with curious concern.

'Watch out, boys!' shouted Dai. 'Incoming! Form a line out!'

The rugby players instantly responded to the command.

Molly had given herself quite a run up. She jogged rapidly to the edge of the stage and hurled herself off the end aiming for the group of men. She sailed through the air in much the same way that a sack of spuds doesn't and fell squarely on top of the Welshmen.

The Rugby players were incredibly strong men. They caught her and managed to hold her aloft for almost a second before the scrum collapsed in a heap of tangled body parts.

'For God's sake, get her off!' came the voice of Dai from the bottom of the pile. 'I can't breathe!'

At that moment Bernie entered the fray. Earlier, they'd made their way down the wide stairway and were waiting in the main entrance lobby just outside the main auditorium. Hearing the ruckus going on inside, Bernie had barged his way through the auditorium entrance doors and was taking in the scene. It was bedlam.

Accompanied by the Best Kept Village judge and the rest of the old folk from the village, they gingerly picked their way through the auditorium and towards the stage. Bernie could see a pile of bodies heaped up close to the stage. A thunderous thigh and calf were protruding from the tangle, and he thought he recognised the lady's shoe dangling from a foot. It was his wife's!

'Molly!' boomed Bernie as he fought his way towards them. He was sweeping aside anyone foolish enough to stand in his way. Bernie was in no way a violent person, but when he thought his wife was in danger, he was not a man to be trifled with. He reached the pile of bodies, and picking up Rugby players as if they were mere bags of clothes, he threw them aside until he had unearthed his wife. He put his arms around her and lifted her free of the wreckage.

'Thank God for that,' groaned a Welsh voice from somewhere under the pile.

'Molly! Molly!' cried Bernie holding her in his arms. 'Are you alright?'

'I'm fine Bernie,' she assured him. 'Really, I am. But you must find Cecilia, she's buried in there somewhere.'

Bernie resumed his manhandling of the Rugby team, throwing more bodies aside.

'Oh no! Not again,' moaned the Welsh voice from the depths.

Presently, Cecilia was extracted from the throng. She was shaken and shocked, but otherwise unharmed.

With the two ladies in tow, Bernie began the assault back to the entrance door, closely followed by the judge and the OAPs.

'I wish that bloke was in our team!' commentated the Welsh voice still buried in the scrum. 'What a player!'

Halfway back across the auditorium, they rendezvoused with Ethel. She had likewise left a trail of carnage in her wake. Anyone remotely entering her range had been ruthlessly dispatched by a swing of her surprisingly lethal tartan handbag.

They battled their way back up the wide stairway. Their intention being to return to the car park and get the hell out of there. The crowd from the auditorium was filtering out and following them up the stairs. They wound their way back along the corridors and arrived back in the VIP lobby area where they had first come in.

In his hiding place in the gents' lavatory, the brigadier could hear the hullabaloo going on in the lobby. Seizing his chance to escape, he cautiously emerged from the cloakroom and blended with the crowd gathered in the foyer. In the confusion, he stealthily made his way towards the exit.

Madam Swish was still reclining on the chaise longue when a multitude of people suddenly swarmed into the lobby. She had no idea where they'd all come from. She rose from the chaise longue and was immediately engulfed by the crowd and swept along. As she looked around her, a few feet away she could see the dome of a balding head bobbing about among the crowd. There were a few wisps of gingery hair combed badly over the top. She knew who that belonged to. She fixed the brigadier's head firmly in her sights. He wasn't going to get away from her that easily.

19.

Sergeant Richards had just changed into his pyjamas and was about to slide into bed next to Linda for an early night, when his emergency phone rang.

'Jesus on a jet ski,' he murmured, cursing his luck. 'Now what?' He knew very well that it was the last day of judging, but he genuinely believed he'd gotten away without any trouble.

'You'd better answer it,' said Linda from under the covers.

Tutting irritably, he padded over to the dresser and picked up his phone. 'Sergeant Richards,' he said bluntly.

'Good evening, Sarge,' said Josh cheerily. 'How are you?'

'Never mind the pleasantries, my lad,' he grumped. 'It's nearly 10pm. I was about to turn in. What the hell is going on?'

'Well, it's like this,' explained Josh. 'I've just had an anonymous call reporting an illegal rave.'

'You what? An illegal rave? In North Norfolk? I'd like to know where!'

'I'm not sure you would, Sarge.'

'What do you mean?' asked Dale suspiciously.

'It's in West Barton. In the village hall. The caller was quite adamant about it.'

'I might have bloody well known,' fumed Dale. 'Okay, I'm on my way.'

'Roger that.'

Dale hung up and tossed the phone back on the dresser. He hurriedly changed back into his uniform and pocketed the phone back in his jacket.

'Sorry about this,' he said to Linda with regret.

'All in the line of duty,' she replied. 'Give 'em hell.'

Dale went downstairs, grabbed the squad car keys and let himself out. He headed off to West Barton – at least it wasn't far away.

*

The party was starting to wind down as the effects of the narcotics were beginning to wear off. Maryam, being medically trained, was the first to realise that something was not at all right. She correctly diagnosed that the whole group attending the party had been exposed to an unknown intoxicant, including herself. Analysing the effects, Maryam's best guess was ecstasy mixed with LSD. She quickly fetched her emergency medical kit from the boot of her car and prescribed herself some pills to help bring her down – and that's when she noticed the pain in her feet.

On closer inspection, she had some severe friction burns to the soles of her feet. She'd obviously sustained them while she was dancing. They were starting to blister. Quickly coming to her senses, she realised some of the others at the party would be far more injured than herself. She immediately called for several ambulances.

*

As Sergeant Richards drove into West Barton, he could see blue lights flashing at the village hall. As he got closer, he saw there were two ambulances pulled up in the car park. They'd obviously only just arrived. As he strode onto the gravelled car park, the front door of the village hall banged open and two paramedics came out, carrying a body on a stretcher.

Dale could see that the person on the stretcher was Reverend Rose. He appeared to be covered in blood and was out cold.

'Is he all right?' Dale asked the paramedic.

'He'll live,' came the reply, 'but he'll have the doozy of a thick head in the morning.'

Another stretcher appeared at the door. Dale saw Cynthia Barrington-Smythe was laid upon it. Her head was jerking from right to left, and her hands and forearms were moving up and down in a robotic fashion.

'Is she having a fit?' he enquired.

'Nope,' responded the paramedic. 'She's having a trip.'

What the hell is going on? Dale wondered.

The patients were placed in one of the ambulances and it shot off at speed, heading for A&E. The remaining paramedics entered the village hall again and returned with two more stretcher-bound casualties. This time, it was Lord Braithwaite and Vincent Kleeb. Both men seemed to be in great pain. Richard was holding his side and groaning, while Vincent's hands covered his groin and he was moaning softly to himself. They were both placed in the second ambulance and whisked away.

Finally, Dr Jahan emerged from the village hall. She was being assisted by her husband on one side and Mrs Chen on the other. She could just about walk, but she, too, was clearly in discomfort. She saw Dale standing in the car park and assumed correctly that he was seeking an explanation.

'What's happened, Doctor?' he asked her.

'We've all been drugged, Sergeant,' was her short reply.

'Drugged? But how? What with?'

'With recreational drugs. Ecstasy, most likely. Maybe LSD. It was in the mulled wine.'

Dale nodded but was puzzled. 'But why?'

'Well, put it this way, Sergeant,' she explained. 'I think we just well and truly blew our chances of winning the Best Kept Village Competition.'

Understanding dawned across Dale's face.

'And now, if you'll excuse me, I'm in rather a lot of pain.'

'Of course,' said Dale. 'Thank you for the explanation.'

Aided by her two assistants, Maryam shuffled off across the street and back to her home.

Dale stood motionless in the car park, trying to take in what he'd just witnessed. Suddenly, he heard the police radio on his belt come to life. It was a general call on the national emergency channel.

'All available units. All available units. Require immediate assistance. Riot in progress in Great Yarmouth. Repeat. Immediate assistance required. All units.'

Dale unhooked the radio from his belt and held it to his mouth. 'Sergeant Richards here, Fakenham district,' Dale acknowledged. 'What is the nature of the riot?'

'Reports of mass brawling between a Welsh rugby club and the Tartan Army.'

'Please advise the exact location.'

'Lapland Nightclub. Great Yarmouth.'

'Did you say Lapland?'

'Affirmative. Lapland Nightclub. Great Yarmouth.'

'On my way. Richards out.'

The sergeant returned to the squad car and started the engine. Once he was out of the village and heading towards the main road, he turned on the flashing lights and siren and put his foot down. As he sped towards Great Yarmouth, he tried to make some sense of the report.

A Welsh rugby team brawling with the Tartan Army?

As far as he knew, there were no Scottish football teams playing in Great Yarmouth at the moment. So, what was that all about? Also, there was something vaguely familiar about the details of the location. He was sure he'd heard the name of the nightclub before. Weren't the East Barton committee organising a trip to Lapland? They were going to the Lapland Christmas Spectacular, which was just a few miles down the road at Thursford, though. Certainly not in Great Yarmouth.

The sergeant began to formulate a theory that didn't bear thinking about. It couldn't be. Could it?

Forty-five minutes later, he screeched to a halt in the car park of the Lapland Nightclub in Great Yarmouth. There were several other police cars already in the vicinity, mostly round the front on the promenade. Many officers were attempting to enter the premises at the main entrance. From where he was standing in the car park, Sergeant Richards noticed a smaller entrance located on the back of the building and decided he'd try to gain entry that way.

He put his helmet on and strapped it tight under his chin. In his left hand, he held his police baton. He kept his right hand free. As he drew closer to the door, he could hear a tumultuous racket coming from inside. He reached his right hand out towards the door handle.

Before he'd even made contact, the door flew open and before he knew it, he'd been dealt a vicious blow over his head. He reeled backwards and, as he did so, a great horde of people began pouring out of the door. He was still seeing stars from the thump to his head. Thank the Lord he'd put his helmet on. As his eyes cleared, all he could see was tartan in front of him. Fearing it was a kilt belonging to a crazed football hooligan, he held an arm up to protect himself.

'I'm so sorry, Sergeant Richards,' came an apologetic Scots voice that he thought he recognised. 'I thought you were one of those stripper-grams dressed as a policeman.'

'What hit me?' exclaimed the sergeant, still a bit dazed. 'Is that you, Mrs McKinley?'

'Aye, it's me,' confirmed Ethel, hiding her handbag behind her back.

'What's going on here?' asked Dale.

'I really couldn't tell you,' said Ethel.

More and more people were pouring out of the door and into the car park. Some of them were still scrapping with one another, but on seeing the presence of the police were thinking better of it.

Out of the corner of his eye, Dale was convinced he just saw Brigadier Faraday skulk out of the door and hoof it across the car park. A woman dressed as a headmistress, wearing fishnet stockings and high heels, came tottering out after him and gave chase. She was hot on his heels and every time she got close, she tried to give him a swipe with her walking cane. The brigadier was protesting bitterly.

'Madam, will you *please* desist?' he shouted frantically, but it only seemed to egg her on.

The brigadier's salvation came to him in the timely

arrival of their minibus. With one monumental last effort, he sprinted towards it, producing an impressive turn of speed for a man of his age. He opened the sliding door and dived in, then hastily locked the door behind him and ducked down behind the seats.

'Step on it!' he shouted to the driver, who dutifully sped the vehicle away to the far end of the large car park. Madam Swish did not pursue them. She turned round forlornly and headed back into the nightclub. Thankfully, he'd finally given her the slip.

The driver turned round in his seat and looked down at the brigadier, who was still crouched down out of sight.

'Evening, squire,' he said with a knowing smile. 'Are we having an eventful evening then?'

'That will do,' warned the brigadier, who'd had quite enough torment for one night.

Sergeant Richards and Ethel were still stood watching people pour out of the back door into the car park. There must have been over a hundred by now. And still they came.

After a short while, the unmistakeable features of Bernie and Molly materialised in the doorway. Cecilia was close behind. Dale and Ethel waved and yelled to get their attention. They waved back and then led their posse of OAPs over to where the policeman and Mrs McKinley were standing.

'Where's Dad?' were the first words out of Bernie's mouth.

'He's not come out yet,' Ethel informed him.

'I hope he's all right,' said Molly, looking worried.

The Aberystwyth 1st XV were beginning to filter out now. One of the heavily built props came through the doorway, carrying an elderly man over his shoulder in a fireman's lift. It was Bill.

Bernie rushed over to the Welshman and grasped his free hand, shaking it vigorously. 'Thank you,' he said gratefully. 'That's my old man you've got there. Is he okay?'

'He's fine. We found him struggling to walk down the corridor, so we offered him a lift. Literally, like!' said the prop genially. He set Bill down on the ground. Bernie thanked him again and led Bill back to the group.

'Are you all safe and sound, Bill?' asked Molly with concern.

'Oh yesh,' nodded Bill with a gummy smile, 'all shafe and shound.'

'Dad,' said Bernie accusingly. 'Where have your teeth gone?'

'Elves,' said Bill.

'Elves?' queried Bernie.

'Thash right. Elves shtole 'em.'

'Elves stole your teeth?'

'Yesh.'

'Are you sure they weren't tooth fairies?' said Molly, laughing.

'Elves,' said Bill defiantly.

Sergeant Richards had taken out his notepad and started writing down the facts of the theft. He now pocketed the notebook again. There was no way he was putting this load of baloney in his report.

The brigadier deemed it safe to return to pick up the rest of the group and gave the say-so to the driver. The minibus drew up alongside the group and they all piled back into the taxi.

'Right,' ordered Sergeant Richards. 'You lot get yourselves back home. I'll stay here and help my colleagues with clearing up this little fiasco. Then, I'll be deciding what I need to put in my report. I'll be seeing you.'

The driver was about to set off when Bernie realised someone was missing. 'Hang on,' he said. 'Where's the judge?'

'I bet he's still inside,' reasoned Molly.

'We'd better go in and get him,' said Bernie, with a sigh.

'Wild horses would not drag me back into that house of ill repute!' the brigadier informed them.

'Look,' said Dale. 'Don't worry. I'll go back in and find him. He can come back with me in the squad car. You lot just get going.'

'Much obliged, Sergeant,' said the brigadier as he leant over and prodded the driver. 'You heard the man. Let's go!'

'Right you are, squire,' muttered the driver. He put the minibus in gear and off they went.

*

The Best Kept Village judge was creeping down a long corridor, clipboard in hand, trying to find the rest of the group. The crowd had largely dispersed and by the time he reached the lobby area, there was hardly anyone about.

Looking at his clipboard, he realised with a sudden panic that with all the pandemonium going on, he hadn't marked any of the assessment forms. He was supposed to be handing them in first thing in the morning. His life wouldn't be worth living if he didn't get it done. He could really do with some assistance from a member of staff to help him fill in his questionnaire. Not that he was going to be giving them a glowing review, mind.

He wondered off at random down a wide corridor and stopped outside a room covered with a purple velvet curtain. 'Hello,' he called from outside.

There was a brief pause. 'Come in,' came an authoritative female voice from within.

The judge went into the room, walked past the tall bookcases and stopped in front of the leather-top desk, holding his clipboard apprehensively.

There was an austere-looking lady sat behind the desk, all dressed in black robes. She looked up from the papers she was reading and took him in with a single glance. She gave him a fleeting smile. 'Do you need help with your homework?' she enquired.

'Oh, yes, most intuitive of you,' replied the judge with a nervous laugh. 'In fact, if I don't get some marks soon, I don't know where I'll be. You see, I haven't managed to score anything all night.'

'I may be able to help you with that,' she said in a sultry voice. 'But first, why don't you help yourself to a drink? There's a fine brandy in the decanter.'

'How kind,' said the judge.

As he walked over to the console table and bent over to pour the brandy, Madam Swish stood up from behind the desk, put on her mortarboard and went to fetch her walking cane.

*

Sergeant Richards conducted a thorough search of the building, taking a good note of all the damage that the proprietors had suffered. The place looked like a bomb site.

No one really seemed to know how the riot had started, although several eyewitnesses claimed it was shortly after the pole on the stage had collapsed. The management had stated that the house dancers were supposed to have been the next act on stage with their three elves routine, but they hadn't turned up for some reason. And they were certainly at a loss to know exactly who the other three mystery performers had been. They hadn't booked anyone with their credentials, although, they had to admit, they'd really brought the house down.

Sergeant Richards interviewed both the Aberystwyth rugby team and the lads who were out on a stag night. Neither contingent were willing to press charges, for the simple reason that none of them wanted the indignity of anyone knowing they'd been roughed up by a plump farmer's wife and an aging Scottish spinster.

By midnight, the sergeant had wrapped things up. There was no sign of the judge, so Dale assumed he must have taken a taxi home. Exhausted, he returned to his squad car and headed for home himself.

Holy Moses, it had been a long day.

20.

The Best Kept Village Competition award ceremony was to be held in Fakenham Town Hall at 6pm on Christmas Eve. The leader of the North Norfolk District Council would be presenting the award. All the committees from the competing villages were due to attend, along with a handful of local dignitaries, representatives from the police force and, of course, a whole host from the clergy.

The *Fakenham Guardian* had been kind enough to erect two A-frame billboards either side of the town hall steps. On the left-hand billboard, there ran a headline decrying the residents of a local village as '*Raving* Mad', while the right-hand billboard informed passers-by of a terrible riot that had recently afflicted Great Yarmouth.

Inside the town hall, the front row of seats had been reserved for the main dignitaries and the competition winners of the previous two years. These being the villages of West Barton and East Barton.

By a quarter to six on Christmas Eve, all the seats in the front row were full. This year, there appeared to be something of a common theme with the previous winning committees. For some reason, many of them seemed to be quite badly injured in one way or another.

The committee from West Barton were sat on the left-hand side, facing the stage. Mr Vincent Kleeb was in the seat on the far left. He had to sit rather awkwardly with his legs stretched out in front of him. This was due to sturdy supports that were wrapped around the top of his thighs and hips. Next to him sat Dr Maryam Jahan. Her feet were heavily bandaged and she had to wear slippers instead of shoes to accommodate them. Lord Richard Braithwaite was sat next in line. He was wincing every now and again from the pain in his ribs and was sat bolt upright due to his upper body being bound up tightly in bandages. Last in line was Mrs Cynthia Barrington-Smythe, who, due to extreme tendon damage, was having to wear a neck brace. Beside her was her son, Michael. He was the only one from the West Barton contingent who was relatively uninjured.

In the middle of the front row sat the various dignitaries. Reverend Rose, looking slightly bashful, was in attendance accompanied by several other local vicars and, of course, the bishop himself. Next there were various councillors, the Mayor of Fakenham, and the Lord Mayor of Norwich. To the side of them were Sergeant Richards and his superior, the chief superintendent.

On the right side of centre, Brigadier Gerald Faraday was noisily inflating a round rubber ring. This was to enable him to sit down in some kind of comfort. Once he'd finished, he placed it on his chair and sat down heavily upon it, making a sound like a squeaky, wet fart. The chief superintendent eyed him with suspicion. Ms Cecilia Dawson, who had also largely escaped any injury, was perched beside her uncle. Mr Bernie Rolls, sporting a black eye, was next. And beside him, exhibiting a collection of smaller all-round bruises, was Mrs Molly Rolls.

Mr Bill Rolls, seated next to her, was looking around the room, smiling toothlessly. His false teeth had not yet been located and were presumed missing in action. (In actual fact, the nightclub's cleaning lady had found them lying neglected on the sofa the next morning. Thinking them some sort of foul new fetish, she had placed them, neatly exhibited, next to the other merchandise in the glass display cabinet).

Last in line was Mrs Ethel McKinley, whose arm was in a sling with an acute tennis elbow injury. As a consequence, she'd had to leave her handbag at home.

Sat further back in the hall, Mr and Mrs Chen, Mr Jahan and many other villagers were in attendance, along with PC Crowther, his partner, Robin, Linda Richards and Mick Granger. Lord Braithwaite had ensured plenty of his staff were present, including Jenkins and several of his groundsmen. All in all, the town hall was packed to the rafters.

There were, however, two ostensibly vacant chairs located in the area reserved for the judges. In the last week, the leader of the council had received two sick notes left in the tray on his desk. One from the West Barton judge, who claimed to be suffering from post-traumatic stress disorder. And the other from the East Barton judge, who had simply stated he was injured. When pressed on the nature of his injury, he had flatly refused to divulge any further details citing personal reasons. The leader would be taking the matter up with them both in the new year.

Other notable absentees were Keith and Jenny Atkins. It being Christmas Eve, they'd had to stay behind to run the pub. They were hoping for a busy night.

At 6pm sharp, the leader of the council emerged from behind the theatre curtain, where he'd been waiting anxiously in the wings, and went to stand behind the lectern in the centre of the stage. An assistant followed closely behind, bearing the coveted Best Kept Village trophy in her arms. Greeting the audience warmly, the leader went on to make an extremely tedious, long and protracted speech, extolling the virtues of the region. He made a point of mentioning all the good work the council had been doing for the area. When he'd finished, there was a smattering of lacklustre applause.

It was time to announce the competition winner. An expectant hush fell across the room. A golden envelope was produced from the leader's inside jacket pocket. He opened it excruciatingly slowly, extracting every last ounce of suspense.

'And the winner of The North Norfolk Best Kept Village Competition is… Bassington!'

'What the bloody blue blazes!' and 'For fuck's sake!'

were the unsporting remarks that could be clearly heard coming from Brigadier Faraday and Mrs Barrington-Smythe respectively, before being drowned out by the applause. They caught each other's eyes momentarily and shook their heads in joint disbelief.

The committee from Bassington were making their way onto the stage amid rapturous applause. The chair of their committee collected the trophy and triumphantly hoisted it above her head with both hands. The crowd clapped loudly, whistling and whooping their congratulations. After a brief thank-you speech, the delegation from Bassington modestly returned to their seats.

What followed next was the longest ten minutes of both the West and East Barton committees' lives. The leader began to read out the remaining results, slowly working his way down the list and ranking each competing village in order of merit. Neither of the Bartons had so far been mentioned. After what seemed an eternity, the leader was nearly done. He read the final result. In bottom place, in joint thirtieth position, and winning a wooden spoon each, were the villages of West and East Barton.

The faces of both the brigadier and Cynthia were set like stone. Simultaneously, they once again turned to look at one another. Cynthia was about to offer up another fearsome profanity, when, much to her own surprise, she gave a snort of laughter instead. The brigadier looked puzzled, but his mouth cracked into a smile and he raised an eyebrow at her.

Cynthia burst into fits of giggles and the brigadier began to chuckle uncontrollably himself. The mirth was contagious and soon all the committee members on both sides were laughing like drains. Reverend Rose couldn't stop himself and he, too, was soon chortling away, wiping tears from his eyes. Sergeant Richards took in the scene and initially looked at them with annoyance, but then the absurdity of it all got to him and he succumbed to it, too. His shoulders started to shake wildly and he was soon in hysterics. The chief superintendent looked at him, gone out.

The award ceremony was breaking up and the crowd started to disperse. Both committees from West and East Barton got to their feet and walked towards each other, still high with mirth. The brigadier went straight over to Cynthia and held her in his gaze.

'Well,' he said with a wry smile, 'we certainly showed them, didn't we?'

'Oh, stop, Gerald!' she said, laughing, and playfully pushed his shoulder.

'I don't suppose you fancy a drink?' he asked.

'What an excellent idea!' She smiled. 'So long as it's not mulled wine.'

'Ah yes, I heard about that,' grimaced the brigadier. 'I assure you we had absolutely nothing to do with it.'

'This time, I believe you,' said Cynthia. 'Besides, I understand you had a few misadventures of your own. By the way, how is your... err...?'

'A bit tender, to be honest,' replied the brigadier, rubbing his behind gingerly.

'Well, I can tell you with great sincerity,' Cynthia informed him, 'that not only did we have nothing to do with sending you to the wrong destination, but we didn't even know that ghastly place existed!'

'Oh, my dear madam, I do not doubt you,' the brigadier assured her.

'Very pleased to hear it.' She smiled again.

'Well, now,' said the brigadier, rubbing his hands together. 'What about that drink? How about The Barton Arms?'

'Perfect,' she said. 'Why don't we all go?'

The brigadier turned to Bernie, who'd been listening in to the conversation. 'Will you do the honours?' he asked him.

Bernie nodded. '*Everyone associated with the Bartons!*' Bernie hollered at the top of his voice. 'We're off to the pub! The Barton Arms! Everyone's invited! *Come on!*'

There was a rousing cheer from all concerned and everyone began to make their way out of the town hall.

Cynthia sought out Reverend Rose and found him putting on his coat ready to leave. 'You will come along with us, won't you, Reverend?' she implored.

'I'd be happy to,' he said with a smile.

'We all feel just terrible about your guitar. I'm going to arrange it so that it's replaced from village funds. We can't have our vicar without his guitar, now, can we?'

'That would be most kind.' He beamed. He'd been down in the dumps ever since the incident. He'd even tried mending it, but it had proved beyond repair. The prospect of a new one certainly put a shine on his day.

The brigadier, meanwhile, went looking for Sergeant Richards. He found him with his wife, Linda, chatting with Josh, Robin and Mick. They all looked up as the brigadier hove down on them. 'I believe I speak for all concerned,' announced the brigadier formally, 'when I say we'd all very much like it if you were to join us for a drink. Would you do us the honour?'

Sergeant Richards looked at him sternly, pretending to be deadly serious.

The brigadier looked worried.

The sergeant relented and broke into a grin. 'You try and keep us away!' Dale replied, smiling. 'We'll be along presently.'

The brigadier beamed at them and declared, 'Good show – what!'

Shortly after, they all filed out of the building and headed for their vehicles. Dale thought he'd better forewarn Keith that he was about to be descended upon, so he fished out his phone and called The Barton Arms.

Keith answered on the second ring. 'The Barton Arms. Merry Christmas! How can I help?'

'Keith, it's Dale. Merry Christmas to you, too!'

'Hello, mate. How are you? Are you dropping in for a drink? It's a bit quiet here.'

'Not for long it won't be!' Dale informed him.

'Eh? How do you mean?'

'Almost the entire population of West and East Barton are on their way to you!'

'Give over! That'd never happen.'

'Trust me, Keith. They're coming. I'll tell you all

about it when I see you. You might want to open about a dozen bottles of wine in readiness.'

'Corkscrew in hand, my friend. That's great. I'll see you in a while then.'

'See you,' said Dale and hung up.

The police were the last to leave the town hall. In the car park, Dale and Linda went over to the squad car. Josh and Robin were in their own car, while Mick drove the dog unit van. They set off in convoy for The Barton Arms.

21.

Keith and Jenny were in a state of high excitement. Keith had been exaggerating when he'd said the pub was a bit quiet. Actually, there was no one in at all. They wanted to make the best impression and greet their guests personally as they arrived, so they had taken Dale's advice and opened a dozen bottles of red and white wine and laid out thirty wine glasses on the bar so that people could help themselves. They'd also poured out several pitchers of beer, a selection of soft drinks and provided a variety of snacks and nibbles. Keith stoked up the fire and put on several more logs, while Jenny went over to the CD player and selected some festive music to play.

They then donned their outdoor jackets and went to stand outside by the entrance door. It was pitch-black outside, but with the interior and exterior fairy lights on, the pub looked festive, warm and inviting. Perfect for a merry Christmas Eve.

Soon enough, the guests started to arrive. The brigadier's vintage Jag was the first car to pull in. He'd given Cynthia, Michael and Cecilia a lift, and they all now alighted from the car and made their way across the car park towards the entrance. Cecilia and Michael led the way, hand in hand and canoodling happily. They paused halfway and, sensing a feeling of guilt, looked back towards Cynthia and the brigadier – as if for approval. They needn't have worried. Both Cynthia and the brigadier nodded jovially at them.

'Run along, you two!' The brigadier smiled at them.

'I won't interfere again – that's a promise,' added Cynthia.

Michael wrapped his arms around Cecilia in a warm embrace and they kissed affectionately, finally free from the vetoes and disapproval they'd endured all year. As they walked into the pub, Keith and Jenny greeted them warmly and wished them both a very merry Christmas.

Following closely behind, Cynthia and the brigadier were beginning a discussion about forming a joint committee. First on the agenda would be to organise a New Year's Eve party. Overhearing the conversation, Keith caught Jenny's eye momentarily and gave her a wink.

'What do you say to hosting that here at the pub?' the brigadier asked Keith.

'I'd be only too happy,' said Keith. 'I look forward very much to hearing your plans. A merry Christmas to you both!'

'Merry Christmas!' chimed the brigadier and Cynthia in unison.

Cynthia hooked her elbow round the brigadier's arm as they entered the pub. 'And then Gerald,' she went on, 'we can start planning for the next competition... but I do suggest each of our villages take it in turn to compete next time, don't you think? Might save a bit of trouble.'

'Good idea,' agreed the brigadier. 'And with both of us on the same committee, we'll trounce those blighters next year!'

They went into the pub as the next cars pulled into the car park. It was bitterly cold outside and Jenny and Keith were starting to feel the chill. Jenny blew into her fingers.

'My hands are like blocks of ice,' she told her husband.

'Mine, too,' said Keith. 'Hang on, though... I think there's some gloves in these coats.'

He began patting various pockets in his jacket before finding the bulge he was looking for. Jenny began the same task and soon located a pair in her jacket, too. They both pulled out the gloves from their pockets and put them on.

Keith's were Lincoln-green, while Jenny's were navy-blue.

'Ooh, that's better,' said Jenny, clapping her hands together for warmth.

Vincent's black limo had just pulled up into the car park and as he ousted himself out from behind the wheel, albeit rather stiffly, he went to open the door for his passenger. As he held the door open, an apparition of tartan slid out from the leather seat and began gathering itself on the gravel driveway. Ethel had thoroughly enjoyed the ride in Vincent's luxurious car. She had never experienced anything quite like it. She could get quite used to it. And she was relishing the attention Vincent was giving her. No one had ever paid her any kind of attention before. She'd never realised quite how charming he was. Well, underneath, at any rate. Keith and Jenny wished them a merry Christmas as they entered the pub.

Richard's 4x4 and Bernie's pickup truck arrived simultaneously, shortly followed by Maryam's Peugeot and Mr and Mrs Chen's small runabout. As they piled into the pub, Bernie was starting a discussion about estate and farm management with Richard and the best way to repair the respective damage they'd each sustained to their horticultural special features. They were both impressed with each other's expertise and knowledge on the subject. Molly and Bill were chatting amiably with Maryam and her husband, when Maryam noticed Bill's missing teeth.

'I have a good friend who's a dentist in Fakenham, you know. If you like, I can get in touch and see about replacing your dentures. Would you like me to?' she asked.

'Oh, yesh. Shank you,' he replied. 'That'd be shuper.'

'I'll get onto it as soon as I can. You might have a new set by New Year's Eve.'

'Shmashing!'

They all passed into the pub, the Chen's last in line, and were all warmly greeted by Keith and Jenny. Many others from both villages also arrived and went inside. The pub was getting pretty full and, from their spot at the entrance, Keith and Jenny could tell from the good-natured chatter they were all having a great time.

Reverend Rose was one of the last to arrive. As he stepped out of his car, he was illuminated by the car park's lighting. Michael and Cecilia came bounding out of the pub to greet him. Cecilia threw her arms around him and gave him a warm hug, while Michael shook his hand vigorously.

The reverend was a little taken aback.

'Oh, Reverend, we can't wait to tell you the good news,' said Cecilia excitedly. 'Michael and I are now formally a couple – and we finally have Gerald and Cynthia's blessing! I can't wait to tell Mum.'

'My, my, that certainly is good news.' The vicar beamed happily at them. He had unofficially taken the couple under his wing all year, secretly allowing them to use the churchyard as their trysting place. He was very fond of both of them and was genuinely thrilled for them.

'And we plan to be wed in the summer,' added Michael, 'and—'

'And we want you to be the one to marry us!' interrupted Cecilia, unable to contain herself. 'Please tell us you will. *Please.*'

'Goodness me, I'd be delighted to, my dear friends! Absolutely delighted!'

Cecilia hugged him again.

'Come on!' said Michael feverishly. 'Let's get back in and tell the others the news!'

The three of them made their way eagerly into the pub, wishing Keith and Jenny a very happy Christmas as they went by. Cecilia made a mental note to ask them later on if they'd be able to cater for the wedding reception. It'd be the perfect location.

Last to get there, the police cavalcade swept into the car park of The Barton Arms and filled the last few parking spaces at the back of the pub. Mick, Josh and Robin got out of their vehicles and stood on the gravel, waiting politely. Dale parked up and was about to switch off the ignition of his squad car when the headlights illuminated something that caught his eye. There was a timber outbuilding behind the pub about the size of a double garage. The headlights were shining on it and Dale noticed the wooden double doors were open and banging about in the wind.

'What is it?' asked Linda, wondering what had caught his attention.

'Oh, nothing much,' replied Dale. 'Keith's left his garage door open by accident, that's all. You go on into the pub with the lads and keep warm. I'll go over and secure those garage doors and be along soon.'

They got out of the car and Linda walked over to where Mick, Josh and Robin were waiting. Once she'd joined them, they set off towards the entrance while Dale went to sort out the banging doors.

Dale left the car headlights on so that he could see

what he was doing. He then made his way over to the outbuilding. Once he'd reached it, he grabbed hold of the left-hand door to secure it. There was an iron bolt screwed to the door, which he slid into a hole in the overhead beam. He started to reach for the right-hand door when curiosity got the better of him. The headlights from the car weren't powerful enough to penetrate into the darkness of the outbuilding, so the sergeant reached for his mobile phone and used the flashlight feature to illuminate the scene.

The first thing he saw was a ride-on mower parked up in the centre of the garage. *Nothing odd about that*, he thought. Towards the back of the garage, a tarpaulin was covering up something that looked like a bicycle. The sergeant went over and lifted the cover. Underneath was a Scrambler motorbike. Now, that was interesting. The hairs on the back of the sergeant's neck began to rise.

He shone the light around the back of the garage. Hanging on hooks screwed to the timber wall were various gardening tools. A spade, a fork, a hoe and some pruning shears. Hanging next to them was a sturdy chainsaw while an empty bottle with a skull-and-crossbones poison sign marked on it was lying on the floor.

The sergeant's heartbeat began to rise. He had to pause and take a deep breath to calm himself. It could all be a coincidence, after all. These were all perfectly normal items that someone could have in a shed or garage. Still…

He cast the light around the outbuilding again. There was a wooden trellis table set up along the right side of the garage wall. Underneath the table was an old-fashioned metal bin with a lid. He noticed that it had round holes drilled into the bottom half of it – it was one of those bins that could be used to burn garden waste.

Hesitantly, the sergeant lifted off the lid and shone the light inside. The bin was full of screwed-up newspaper, ready to use as tinder to start a fire. The sergeant put his hand in the bin and rummaged around. Soon, he found an item he'd been dreading to discover. His hand closed around a small jar. As he lifted it out, there was the unmistakeable round yellow smiley face logo on it that everyone knew to be associated with recreational drugs. After a little more searching, he pulled out an envelope that was still sealed. He hastily ran a finger under the seam and opened it. Inside were detailed directions to the Lapland Christmas Spectacular venue, located just a few miles away down the main road.

Dale felt the pit of his stomach fall. Here in front of him was all the evidence required to charge the offenders and wrap up the case – with just one slight drawback. The offenders happened to be some of his best friends. Sometimes, he hated being a policeman. It was his legal obligation to apprehend and charge Keith and Jenny Atkins. Two of the nicest, most genuine people he'd ever met. *Oh, dear God*, he lamented. *On Christmas Eve, too*. It didn't bear thinking about.

With gloom and dread in his heart, he pocketed

the jar and envelope and trudged back out of the outbuilding. He turned off the flashlight on his phone and closed the right-hand door of the garage, flipping the latch to hold it in place.

As he walked slowly back to the squad car, he wondered what could possibly have possessed Keith and Jenny to do such a thing. Switching the ignition off and locking the car, he turned to face the pub. As he gazed at the happy shining faces of the people through the windows, his question was succinctly answered for him.

The folk inside the pub were enjoying their drinks and merrily chatting away with one another. Villagers, who, only days ago, would have gladly danced on each other's graves were now smiling and laughing together like lifelong friends. It felt good.

The sergeant thought hard on how this eventuality could have happened. Could it be, he wondered, that by actually forcing the opposing committees into abject failure, Keith and Jenny had successfully brought the two sides together, united by their shared misfortune? Because *together* they most certainly were. And the proof of that success was now staring him in the face. The feuding was over. And surely that was no bad thing.

The more Dale thought about it, the more he realised that Keith and Jenny's plan was a work of sheer and utter genius. Not only had they stopped the feuding and brought the two villages together, but, by the looks of it, they were going to be running a very profitable pub in the very near future. It was impressive.

Dale walked round the corner to the front of the pub where Keith and Jenny were still stood waiting for him by the entrance. Dale's face was expressionless as he walked closer to them. Keith and Jenny turned towards him as he approached and saw that his face was set as hard as granite.

'Is everything all right, Dale?' asked Jenny with concern.

In response, the sergeant slowly reached into his pockets and withdrew the two items he'd found in the outbuilding. In the palm of his left hand, he held the pill bottle and, in his right, the envelope with the directions. He held the items up so that they could be clearly seen.

For a brief moment, Keith and Jenny looked dumbly at the items, but then the colour drained from their faces as they realised what they were looking at. They both looked up at Dale with imploring eyes, but his face remained impassive.

Eventually, the sergeant spoke. 'I think you two had better come with me,' he said sombrely.

Keith and Jenny looked crestfallen. Tears were starting to well in Jenny's eyes.

'We'll come quietly,' whispered Keith dejectedly. 'But I just want you to know… we never meant anyone any real harm.'

'We just wanted to stop the arguing and fighting,' sobbed Jenny, 'and try and save our pub.'

The sergeant replaced the items back in his pockets and took a step forward, so that he was standing in between Keith and Jenny. He raised the palms of his hands up to silence them both. 'I think,' he said again, 'that you two had better come with me.'

He then reached out with widespread hands and placed an arm around each of Keith and Jenny's shoulders. 'Because...' he continued, giving them a sly grin, 'I want to be the first... to buy you a drink! You absolute *beauties*!'

Keith and Jenny goggled at him, absolutely dumbfounded.

'Whaaat?' queried Keith, unsure he'd heard right.

Jenny was wiping the tears from her eyes and looking up at Dale uncertainly.

'You did it!' exclaimed Dale, smiling broadly now. 'You only went and bloody well *did it*! You clever, clever people! You've brought them altogether! You've achieved the impossible! You pair of absolute stars!'

Keith and Jenny were smiling back at him now and beginning to laugh with relief.

'But... but... what now?' spluttered Jenny.

'Well, stop me if I'm wrong,' said Dale heartily, 'but I'd say it was high time we got this party started! Don't you?'

They nodded vigorously.

He gave their shoulders a gentle squeeze and together they strode into The Barton Arms to the rapturous sound of a loud and joyful cheer.

Acknowledgements

I'd like to thank my wife, Lois, for her horticultural advice, Gill Baguley for the cover illustration and anyone else who has helped or inspired me along the way.